Be a

Triple Threat !

ORCA
YOUNG
READERS

Triple Threat

Eric Walters and
Jerome "Junk Yard Dog" Williams

ORCA BOOK PUBLISHERS

National Library of Canada Cataloguing in Publication Data

Walters, Eric, 1957-
Triple threat / Eric Walters and Jerome Williams (Junk Yard Dog).

(Orca young readers)
ISBN 1-55143-359-1

I. Title. II. Series.

PS8595.A598T75 2004   jC813'.54   C2004-905878-9

Library of Congress Control Number: 2004113950

Summary: The eighth installment in Eric Walters' popular basketball
series for young readers with a contribution by NBA player Jerome "Junk
Yard Dog" Williams.

Free teachers' guide available.

Orca Book Publishers gratefully acknowledges the support for its
publishing programs provided by the following agencies: the Government
of Canada through the Department of Canadian Heritage's Book
Publishing Industry Development Program (BPIDP), the Canada Council
for the Arts, and the British Columbia Arts Council.

Cover design by Lynn O'Rourke
Cover and interior illustrations by John Mantha

In Canada: **In the United States:**
Orca Book Publishers   Orca Book Publishers
Box 5626, Stn.B   PO Box 468
Victoria, BC Canada   Custer, WA USA
V8R 6S4   98240-0468

07 06 05 04 • 6 5 4 3 2 1
Printed and bound in Canada

To quote my friend, Steve Coleman, this book is dedicated to all those who take the time to help others 'rise up.' —*EW*

I dedicate this book to all my fans in the Dogg Pound, for all your support in making my dreams a reality. —*JYD*

I

"Man, it is so hot," Kia said as she collapsed onto the front lawn of my house.

"It's hot," I agreed. I walked off the driveway—the court—and sat down beside her, using the basketball as a stool.

"It's not just hot, Nick. It's so hot that the pavement is practically melting. So hot that moving almost hurts. So hot that I just want to lie down in the shade until it's not so hot anymore."

"Like I said, it's hot."

"I don't want it to be hot anymore."

"Kia, you hate the cold. You spend the whole winter doing nothing but complaining about how cold you are. Now that it's not cold you do nothing but complain about the heat. Aren't you ever happy?"

"When I'm happy I'll let you know."

"I can't make it cold, but do you want something cold to drink?" I asked.

"Yeah, that would be great, but how about if we wait until after I beat you."

We'd had four games of one-on-one. I'd won all four. Kia was a good player—the best girl player I knew. Heck, she was probably the best ten-year-old female player in the whole city.

We'd played together for years and years, and over that time we'd always been pretty even. But not the last few weeks. Not today. Today I was hot in a whole different way.

"Do you really want to play another game?" I asked.

"Of course I want to play," she said.

"But I thought it was so hot."

"It is. So hot that the only thing I'm willing to do that doesn't involve sitting in the shade is playing some basketball."

"How about if we get that drink first?" I suggested.

"No. First I beat you and then we get a drink."

"A hot drink?" I asked.

"Why would I want a hot drink?" Kia asked.

"If I keep playing as well as I'm playing, it'll be winter before you beat me and you'll be wanting a hot drink because you'll be complaining about the cold."

"Funny, very funny."

Kia got up from the lawn and sauntered onto the driveway. I got up off the ball, picked it up and followed after her.

The second my shoes hit the blacktop I felt the heat radiating out of the pavement. It felt like the asphalt was actually squishing a little bit under my feet. On the grass, in the shade, it was hot. Here on the driveway, in the mid-day sun, it was *so* hot. Not that I was going to admit that to Kia. If she wanted to play, we'd play.

"You want first ball?" she asked.

"Loser gets first ball so I guess that's you... again."

She snarled at me. Taunting Kia probably wasn't that smart a thing to do. But what did it matter? Part of me even wondered if I should throw the game. The sooner she won the sooner we could go in and get a cold—

"And don't you even think about throwing the game," she said, reading my mind.

If anybody but Kia had done that I would have been shocked and surprised. Kia could read my mind. And I could read hers. Best friends are like that, and we'd been best friends forever.

"If you're so smart," I said, "what am I thinking right now?"

"You're thinking that the last four games were a fluke and you can't make it five in a row."

I smiled slightly. I knew there was no fluke. I was pretty sure I could beat Kia almost every time, and it wasn't because I was better than her—well not that much better. It was just that I knew how to beat her.

Kia was a better shooter than me and as good at dribbling and driving. She was even a little bit taller than me. What I had was size. I outweighed her by enough that I could just set up, back her into the key and push against her until I was right under the hoop for an easy basket. That one advantage was enough to win.

"You going to play real basketball this time?" Kia asked.

"What is that supposed to mean?"

"Real basketball. Driving the net, breaking somebody down on the dribble, shooting the ball from outside. You know, real basketball."

"I'll do all of those things. Once you stop me from doing what I'm doing."

Coach Barkley—our rep team basketball coach—always said that basketball was a very easy game. All you had to do was figure out what worked and keep doing it until it didn't work anymore.

I tossed Kia the ball. She began dribbling. It was the strangest thing—the ball didn't "ping" when it hit the pavement as much as give a little "squishy" sound. It was too hot for basketball. I wanted that drink more than I wanted to play. It was my time to try to read Kia's mind.

"Want to call it a draw?" I asked.

"We haven't even started."

"I noticed."

Kia hated losing. Not that I liked it, but she hated it with a passion. Calling it a draw would give her—and me—a way out of having to play another game.

"Before the game starts is the best time to call it a draw. What do you say we call the fifth game a tie?"

She picked up the ball. "I could win, you know."

"You could. And so could I. If we play, somebody wins and somebody loses. If we call it a draw, we both win."

"How do you figure that?" Kia asked.

"Because we get out of the sun and into my air-conditioned house and have something cold to drink. Doesn't that sound like a win-win situation?"

Kia didn't answer.

"Well?"

She tossed me the ball. "I'll let you off this time. Let's go inside."

"Gee, thanks ... really appreciate it," I said sarcastically.

I was hit by a wonderful wave of cool as I opened the front door. I inhaled deeply and let the air soak into my lungs. "Doesn't that feel good."

"Almost as good as that cold drink you promised me."

I dropped my basketball into the wicker basket behind the door and we headed into the kitchen. I half expected my mother to be in there, but the room was empty. That meant she was in the basement in her little office, working. She was a reporter with the local paper and did most of her writing down there at the computer.

"What do you want?" I asked as I opened up the fridge.

"What you got?"

"Everything." I was hardly exaggerating.

My mother always made sure we had a fridge stocked with drinks and lots and lots of snacks—healthy snacks. For most people the words "healthy" and "snack" didn't go together, but my mother made it work. Carrot sticks, oatmeal muffins, granola bars, power bars, apples and bananas and other assorted fruits and vegetables. My house was the hangout not just for Kia and me, but for all of our friends.

Kia reached in and grabbed the pitcher of lemonade. I grabbed a Coke.

"Hope your mother doesn't walk in now."

"I'm allowed to drink Coke," I protested. I was allowed to drink Coke, just not as often as I'd like, and certainly not after playing ball and sweating like a pig.

"With so many choices, why would you choose that?" Kia questioned.

"I like Coke."

"You also like lemonade and power drinks and water. You know that practically nothing's better for you than water when you've been sweating hard."

"Now you sound like my mother."

"And what exactly is wrong with that?" my mother asked as she walked into the room.

"Nothing, I guess, if you're forty years old."

"You better be careful about who you're calling forty," my mother said.

My mother wasn't going to be forty for a few years. She liked to point that out to my father, who had just turned forty.

"So how are you two enjoying summer vacation?" my mother asked.

"I'm bored," Kia said.

"Bored!" I exclaimed. "It's only the third day of vacation and you're bored?"

"There's nothing to do," she said.

"There's lots of things to do."

"So far we haven't done any of them. All we've done is play ball on your driveway."

"I never heard you complain about being bored playing basketball," I said.

"We're not playing basketball. We're playing one-on-one. It's getting old."

I wanted to say that losing was what was getting old for her, but I was a little too smart for that.

"Why don't you invite somebody else over to play?" my mother suggested.

"There isn't anybody else to invite over," I said. "Everybody's away."

"Everybody?" my mother asked in that "are you sure?" tone that mothers use.

"He's not kidding," Kia said. "Mark, Jamie, Jordan, Paul, Tristan, Ashton ... everybody."

"They're all over the place. Jordan's family has gone back to Europe for a holiday. Ashton's down in New York. Jamie's at a baseball tournament in Michigan," I said.

"I thought it seemed pretty quiet around here the last couple of days," my mother said. "I guess it could be worse, though. At least you two are here now and going away at the same time."

Our parents tried to coordinate our holidays so that we both went away at the same time, even though we were going to different places.

"Maybe you two should hit the recreation center," my mother suggested.

"Are you through working for the day?" I asked.

"Lots more to do."

"But if you have work to do ... then what?"

"How about you grab something to eat and you walk there?" my mother answered.

"Walk ... by ourselves?"

"It's not that far."

"It's not. It's just that you don't like us to go there by ourselves," I said.

"You're getting older. I think it'll be okay. Don't you?"

"Of course!" I exclaimed. "I thought we were old enough last year when you wouldn't let me go there."

"Last year you weren't old enough. This year you are. So are you going to go?"

I looked over at Kia. She nodded.

"Right after we get some food."

"I can make you something to eat." My mother paused. "Actually, while I'm making the food, you have a chance to go upstairs and do your reading."

"I can do it later on, before bedtime."

"That's what you said yesterday, and you didn't do it. You fell asleep."

"You can't blame me for falling asleep," I reasoned. "I was tired."

"Nobody is blaming you. I just would prefer that you did your reading before you were tired."

"I don't know why I have to read at all."

"I just want to make sure you read every day, the way your teacher suggested on your report card."

"He suggested what?" Kia questioned.

"That Nick read every day. Didn't Nick tell you?" my mother asked.

"I don't tell her everything," I said. There were some things I didn't want her to know.

"I tell you everything," Kia said.

"It's nothing. One line out of a great report card."

"It was a great report card and it wasn't like Mr. Roberts was saying anything bad. He just thought it would be good if you read for twenty minutes every day throughout the summer."

"He probably wrote that on everybody's report card," I said.

"He didn't write it on mine," Kia said.

"But he did write it on Tim's and Jessie's and every one of the guys I spoke to," I said.

"Maybe he just wrote it on all the boys' report cards," Kia suggested.

"Why would he write it just on the boys' report cards?" my mother asked.

"Some of the boys—not all of them—aren't into reading that much."

"That makes no sense. Aside from reading being fun to do, you need it for your future. What can somebody become if they can't read?" my mother asked.

"How about a professional basketball player?" I suggested.

"Come on, Nick, you know better than to say that," my mother said.

"She's right," Kia agreed. "All those guys went to university and some were even honor students. If they couldn't read well, they couldn't have done that."

Sometimes having Kia here was like having a second mother.

"I can read," I said, realizing that that argument was going nowhere.

"We know you can read. It's just that practice makes perfect. Just because you know how to play basketball doesn't mean you don't go to practices to get better at it."

"How about if I just go outside and practice my jump shots instead?" I asked.

"Nicholas," my mother said, using my whole name, which was never a good sign, "like it or not, agree or not, you're still going to be reading for twenty minutes every day."

"You're probably right ... I won't like it or agree with it but I'll do it."

"I never mind reading," Kia said. "How about if

we both take a twenty-minute break, sip something cold and read?"

I shrugged. There was no point in arguing anymore. I stomped up the stairs to my room, Kia close on my heels. I flopped down on my bed and grabbed the book I was reading off my night table.

"What are you reading?" Kia asked.

I held up the book. "Matt Christopher."

"Is it a good book?"

"His books are always good. Nobody can write sports books like him. I always feel like I'm right there, watching or even playing."

"I'm confused. If you like his books, why are you kicking up such a fuss about reading?" Kia asked.

"It's summer. Summer isn't for reading."

"I didn't know reading had a season."

"Everything has a season. For reading it's the school year. During the summer the only thing I should be reading is the TV guide, the sports section if there's been a big game or a trade, and the back of the cereal box when I'm eating breakfast."

"That's all reading," Kia said.

"Could you tell my mother that? Sometimes I think she listens to you more than she does me."

"Still ... why limit yourself? Reading is fun, so why not just do it?"

"I got better things to do," I said.

"Such as?"

"Playing ball, watching TV or movies, playing video games ... lots of stuff."

"I think reading is one of the best things to do," Kia argued. "I always read every day."

"Good for you. How about if you grab a book and start reading and stop talking."

Kia ambled over to the bookshelf and started browsing. There were hundreds of books for her to choose from ... hundreds of really good books ... I knew that because I'd read every one of them at least once.

I opened up my book to the spot where I'd placed the bookmark. I scanned down the page, finding the exact spot where I'd stopped, and began reading ... this was a good book.

2

The recreation center wasn't that far away—at least by car. Driving took only about five minutes. By foot it was a lot farther and took a lot longer. I guess that was the price of freedom. We were also off to a later start than we had planned. I'd become lost in the book and read for close to forty minutes before I realized it.

Even though we had to walk, having permission to go was still a big improvement. My parents—and Kia's parents—had always been clear that it wasn't a place we could go on our own. It wasn't just the distance, but also that it was on the border between our neighborhood and one that wasn't "quite as nice"—that's how my mother always said it. That meant poorer and tougher. I wasn't sure why she'd had a sudden change in her thinking, but I wasn't going to argue.

My mother tended to be overprotective. Sometimes I thought that if she had her way, she'd still be walking me to school in the morning, cutting up my food at meals, and tucking me into bed by eight each night. It wasn't like I was some stupid little kid. I was eleven.

I liked the rec center. I'd taken swimming lessons there every summer. I'd played house league soccer out on the fields. I'd even hung around the playground. Of course all those activities were under the watchful eyes of at least one of my parents.

The center was big and it had almost everything. Besides the pool, playground and soccer field, it also had an ice rink, skateboard park, some tennis courts and, most important, a big beautiful outdoor basketball court. And not just any court. It was one of the best-kept, fanciest courts I'd ever seen. I'd never really done anything more than take a couple of shots there before. It was always busy with the big kids— high school and older—playing ball. I liked to watch them play. Watching wasn't as good as playing, but it was okay. It's funny … like when I was reading that book, it was almost like watching somebody play.

Kia and I had packed our bathing suits, towels and some snacks. The plan was to go for a swim. The cold water would feel so good. I'd also packed a surprise—my very, very favorite basketball. I was hoping that after the swim, if the court wasn't busy, maybe we could shoot around a little. Of course I knew playing ball was a long shot, but what did I have to lose? Some of the best players in the whole city sometimes played there. On a day as hot as today, maybe watching might even be better.

"It is so hot," Kia said.

"We're not going there again. But we are going there," I said, pointing at the rec center in the distance.

The park surrounding the center looked deserted. The tennis courts were empty, the soccer field grass was brown and burned out, and there were only a couple of little kids on the swings at the playground, their parents sitting on the benches in the shade, watching.

"Do you think anybody's playing ball?" Kia asked.

"Not having X-ray eyes, it's a little hard to tell." The basketball court was on the far side of the center, hidden behind the pool.

"X-ray vision? I never figured you had any super-human powers," Kia said. "Let's have a look."

We circled around the building. To my surprise the basketball court was completely empty!

"Do you want to play some ball?" I asked.

"I'd love to but we don't have a ball."

"That's where you're wrong." I tapped my back-pack. "Guess what's in my pack?"

"You brought a ball?"

"You never know when a basketball game might break out...although I thought you were tired of playing one-on-one."

"Tired of playing on your driveway. Let's have a game and then go for a swim. It'll make the swim even better."

"Sure. We can play. I'll take it easy on you."

Kia muttered something under her breath. I hadn't heard her but figured I knew exactly what she'd said.

The court was surrounded by a high wire fence. We walked in through the little gate at the side. The court was asphalt, but it had been dyed a greenish color to look like the floor at the Boston Gardens where the Celtics played. On a day like today, with the sun beating down, it was more than just decorative; it was cooler than standing on blacktop. At both ends of the court were two perfect Plexiglas backboards. The rims were level and had wire meshes. This was one beautiful court.

We dropped our backpacks against the fence and I pulled out my ball—my favorite ball. It was leather, NBA size and weight, official colors of the Raptors and autographed by one of their players.

"Wow," Kia said when she spied the ball. "What are we going to do with that?"

"Play ball."

"You never play with this one. What's the special occasion?"

"Nothing special. What good is a ball if you don't use it?" I asked in reply.

"If that's true then why have you been keeping it in your room in that trophy case for the last year?"

"I changed my mind."

What had changed was that I thought Kia needed a boost and I figured this might be it. Besides, having a basketball and not using it was like owning a car but never driving it.

Kia took the ball from me. She bounced it a couple of times. "Nice feel. Shame though."

"What's a shame?" I asked.

"Shame you're using your special ball to lose."

"Big talk. Take it out."

Kia smiled. "I'll take it out and then put it in ... in the hoop." She tossed me the ball. "Check."

I tossed it back to her. "Ball in."

She started dribbling. I knew her moves. I knew what she would try to do to beat me, and I'd be ready. She knew me as well, the best ways to beat me. Playing against somebody you knew this well was as much a mind game as a physical game.

"So you coming out to get me?" Kia asked as she continued to dribble outside the three-point line.

"Nope. I'm happy here," I said, one foot in the paint, one outside, on an angle that would force her to her left—her weak side.

"Hey!" yelled out a loud, deep voice.

I turned toward the voice and Kia used that split second to slip by me and put up an easy lay-up for a basket.

"That's not fair!" I exclaimed.

"Can't let the crowd interfere with your—"

"What do you think you're doing?" called out the same voice.

This time we both looked. There were three guys—big teenager, high school guys—walking toward us.

21

They were all dressed in basketball gear, right down to headbands on their shaved heads. One of them was white and the other two were black. All three were big, but the white guy was really big. Behind them, sitting in the shade of a large tree, were another dozen or so guys. We hadn't noticed them.

The three guys strolled up and in through the gate.

"What you kids doing?" the largest of the three asked.

"Just playing ball," I said nervously.

"You can't play ball here," he snarled. "Go away."

"Sure, no prob –"

"Why can't we play here?" Kia demanded.

"Because it's our court," said the second guy.

I started to walk over to get my bag when Kia grabbed me by the arm.

"Hang on. What do you mean, your court?" she asked. "It belongs to the city."

"It may belong to the city, but we own it. The three of us. We earned this court by being the best there is. We're the three-on-three champions of River Grove Recreation Center."

"Congratulations," I said, trying to figure out what else I could say.

22

"Yeah, gee, congratulations," Kia said. "The champions of a whole rec center…real impressive. We were the champions of the whole city last summer. We won Hoop It Up at the exhibition last year."

"I didn't know they had a division for babies," one of them said, and the other two laughed.

I looked over anxiously toward the gate. What I saw didn't make me feel any better. All of the other guys had gotten up off the grass and were hanging on the fence, looking and listening in and laughing.

"We were just playing here because we didn't know," I apologized.

"You weren't even on the court," Kia added.

"So what? You got a house, little girl?" the guy demanded.

What sort of a question was that?

"Yeah, of course I have a house."

"And are you there right now?"

"Of course not," Kia said. "I'm here."

"Even if you're here, it's still your house. Wouldn't you be mad if I just showed up in your house when you weren't home, without an invitation or your permission? You'd call the cops, right?"

"Yeah."

"Well, this is our house. Even when we're not on it, you don't come in without our permission."

"We didn't know," I said. "Do you think that maybe we could play a little?"

"Too late. Can't break in and then ask for permission. Beat it!"

"Kia, we've got to get going and—"

"Yeah, Kia, you better listen to your boyfriend," the third guy taunted.

"He's not my boyfriend! Just because you can play some ball doesn't mean you can chase people off the court who want to play, you know."

"You tell 'em, girl!" one of the guys at the fence yelled out, and the others started laughing.

The three guys didn't look like they thought it was that funny. Actually, it wasn't. This was no laughing matter, and getting people who were big and angry even angrier was not a good strategy.

"Maybe she has a point," the biggest guy said.

"She does?" asked one of his friends. He sounded as surprised at his words as I was.

He shrugged. "Maybe we shouldn't just chase them off. Fair is fair."

Those weren't words that I expected to be coming out of his mouth.

"If they want to stay, all they have to do is play … play us."

"What?" I asked in shock.

"You think you can play ball. You beat us and you can rule the court."

"We can't play you," I said in disbelief.

"Why not, no guts?" he laughed.

"Like it takes a lot of guts to bully a couple of kids who are half your age," Kia said.

"Don't matter how big or how old you are. You play, you win, you rule. You want to play us or what?"

"You're like twice our size. How fair is that?" Kia asked.

"Yeah, but we're only the champions here at River Grove and you're the champions of the whole city, so doesn't that make it even?" he chided.

"Come on, get real," Kia said. "We won against kids our age."

"Then maybe you should go and find some kids your age and go someplace else to play. This court is for the big boys."

"Big jerks," Kia snarled.

"Kia, cool it," I said under my breath.

"You may not have noticed, or can't count, but there are only two of us," Kia said.

25

"More like two halves. Either way, though, you want to be here, you have to earn it. Come back when you have a third player. You can get anybody you want. Anybody! But until then ... scram!"

Suddenly he reached out and grabbed my ball away from Kia. Without any warning, and before we could even think to react, he dropped the ball to the ground and gave it a tremendous kick. It soared up and up and up and over the fence. It landed in the parking lot and bounced out into the street, just clearing the roof of an oncoming car and narrowly missing a truck. Then it rolled down the street, straight toward a city bus. In seconds the ball disappeared beneath the bus and there was a huge *bang*! The bus just kept going. There on the road—all squashed flat—was my ball! It had been run over by the back wheels.

"My ball!" I screamed.

"Ain't much of a ball now!" somebody joked. "More like a pancake!"

The three guys, and those standing by the fence, all broke into laughter.

"Nice shot!" somebody yelled out.

"Way to go!" another voice screamed.

"Now, the two of you better leave through the gate

27

or that basketball isn't the only thing I'm going to boot over the fence!" the big guy threatened.

I stood there, open-mouthed, shocked, unable to think or talk or react. Kia grabbed me by the hand. "Come on, Nick, let's go."

I trailed after her. She reached down to grab the two backpacks and led me out through the gate. I felt stunned and just stumbled forward. I heard lots more laughter as we left. I didn't look back. I wanted to get away as fast as possible. I couldn't understand. Why had he done that? How could anybody be that mean? I just didn't understand.

3

I stared at the remains of the ball in my hands. Kia had run onto the street to rescue it. There wasn't much to rescue. Purple rubber roadkill.

"I can't believe he did that," I said. We stood there, by the rec center but out of sight of the basketball court.

"The guy is a big, mean jerk. I hate bullies, just hate them," Kia said. "I'm sorry."

"So am I."

"No, I mean I'm sorry because this was my fault."

"How do you figure that?" I asked.

"This wouldn't have happened if I'd just kept my mouth shut and we'd left."

"Kia, you're my best friend, but you can *never* keep your mouth shut. You know that."

"I know, but this time I should have. You can't reason with a bunch of stupid gorillas like that."

"Reasoning is one thing. Insulting them is another. But still, it wasn't your fault. You weren't the one who did that to my ball."

"But if I'd just shut up, maybe he wouldn't have kicked it over the fence. I'm sorry ... that's all."

I shook my head slowly. "I don't get it. What makes people like that tick? What's the big thrill of picking on somebody half your size and age?"

"I don't know, but if I was twice his size I'd find out pretty quick," Kia said with a laugh. "I'd kick his ball, then his butt, over that fence."

"No you wouldn't."

"Why wouldn't I?" Kia said.

"Because you're not a bully. I've never seen you pick on anybody and I don't think you're going to start now. It's not you."

"If I was twice as big as him, maybe I'd start."

I opened up my backpack and carefully put the flattened ball inside.

"What do you think your parents are going to do when you tell them what happened?" Kia asked.

"I'm hoping not to find out because I'm not going to tell them."

"Why not? Maybe they can call the police or your dad can come down here or—"

"None of that is going to happen. I don't want them to know anything about it. If we tell them about those guys, they'll probably decide that we shouldn't be coming here by ourselves."

"I hadn't thought about that. Knowing how over-protective your mother is, she may not let you go anywhere by yourself again."

"Don't laugh. If my parents won't let me go, do you think your parents will?" I asked.

"Even if you don't tell them, what are your parents going to say when they see the ball?" Kia asked.

"I'm going to put it in my closet where they're not going to see it."

"If you really don't want them to see it, wouldn't it be better if you just tossed it out?" she suggested.

"I guess it would, but I can't do that." I closed the zipper. "It was a present from my dad, and it was signed and everything."

"I guess it still is signed," Kia commented.

"Autographed roadkill."

"That's too bad. If your parents do see it, or they ask you where it is when they don't see it in the display case, what are you going to tell them?" Kia asked.

31

"I'm going to tell them that it was run over by a bus. I'm going to tell them the truth ... or at least half of the truth. I'm just not going to tell them what caused the ball to get under the bus to begin with."

"I guess it's just our secret." Kia paused. "Do you still want to go swimming?"

"I don't think so. You?"

"Nope. You know what I'd really like to do?"

"What?" I asked.

"I'd like to go back on that court and beat those guys."

"Yeah, like that's going to happen. They're like seventeen years old."

"Maybe older."

"It doesn't matter if they're seventeen or twenty-seven or seventy-seven because—"

"Actually, if they were seventy-seven we could probably take them," Kia said, cutting me off. "Senior citizens we could take."

"But they're not and we can't take them."

"We could if we were seventeen."

"Great, let me mark that on my calendar. In seven years we'll go back and show them. How about if we just forget it until then, okay?"

32

"I don't think I can forget it. I just want to get even for what they did."

"Like I said, that's not going to happen. They won and we lost. Forget it."

"I don't want to lose and I don't want them to win. Bullies shouldn't be winners," Kia said. "Wouldn't it be something if we could go back and play them and beat them?"

"That would be amazing," I had to admit. "Not possible but amazing."

"I'd love to see the look on their faces, being beat by some kids. And then we'd kick them off the court."

I started to laugh. "That would be even more amazing."

"Just after we scored the winning basket, I'd stroll on over to that big goof and tell him to get his sorry butt off *our* court ... get out of *our* house."

"And then I'd take his basketball and kick it over the fence and hope that it would get run over by a bus," I added.

"That would be the perfect final touch," Kia agreed.

I could picture it all in my mind—the ball soaring up and over the fence ... I could only hope that a bus would be coming along. Of course, my mind was the only place it was going to take place. We had no chance of beating them.

"Who's the best player you know?" Kia asked.

"I don't know. Jordan. Maybe Jamie. Mark's the best shooter."

"I don't mean kids our age. I mean anybody."

"Well, probably Coach Barkley." Coach Barkley was our rep ball coach. He had been a star in college and even played in the NBA before a knee injury forced him to retire.

"He was really good," Kia agreed. "But he's old. He's like forty. Besides, with his bad knee he wouldn't be good enough to help us beat those three."

"Kia you have to forget it. We're not going to play those guys. Even if Coach Barkley had two good legs, even if he was younger, even if he'd agree to play, we still couldn't use him."

"Why not?" Kia asked.

"Because he'd tell our parents what happened and they can't find out about any of this, remember?"

"Oh, yeah, that's right."

"So let's just forget about it ... okay?"

She didn't answer right away.

"Okay?"

She shrugged. "Sure, I'll forget it. What are we supposed to say to your mother about today?"

"Nothing. Just tell her we went to the center and hung around."

"We could say we went swimming," Kia suggested.

"Let's just not tell her anything. Lying to my mother is like lying to you. It doesn't work. So the less we say the better."

"If you think that's the best way, I'll keep my mouth closed."

"It is the best way, but that would be a first."

"What would be a first?" Kia asked.

"You keeping your mouth closed."

"You better apologize or I'm going to keep my mouth closed for the rest of the day."

"Okay, okay, I'm sorry...sorry that you have trouble keeping your mouth shut."

Kia reached over and slapped me on the side of the head. I laughed and skipped out of range before she could hit me again.

"You jerk!"

"So now I'm a jerk too? You're just lucky you don't have a basketball or I'd kick it over a fence."

"You're lucky I don't kick you over a fence!" she yelled playfully.

"Hey, you said you'd keep your mouth shut, so how about keeping it shut! I could use the peace and quiet!"

Kia started laughing and I laughed with her.

"So what would you do if I really didn't talk to you?" she asked.

"I told you...have some peace and quiet. You coming to my place for dinner?"

"What are you having?" she asked.

"Not sure."

"Check, and I'll find out what we're having for dinner at my place. Let's go to whichever house has the best meal happening."

"Now that's a plan," I said.

We continued to walk along. I was wanting to forget about what happened, but I couldn't. Those guys were just plain mean. Mean and scary.

Even worse than thinking about what had happened was thinking that I knew Kia well enough to know that she wasn't going to let this go. If there was any way—*any* way—that she could get back at those guys, she was going to do it.

One of the reasons I was glad to have Kia as my friend was that she would be a really bad enemy to have.

"Isn't that your dad's car in the driveway?" Kia asked.

"Yeah ... it is. Wonder what he's doing here."

"He lives there, remember?"

"I mean, what is he doing here this early. He's not usually home until way later."

"Only one way to find out," Kia said.

4

"Hello!" I yelled as we raced through the door.

"Nick! Kia! That's great that you're both here," my father said as he came to meet us at the front door.

"We're here, but why are you home so early?" I asked.

"Five o'clock isn't that early."

"It is for you," I said. "You haven't been home for supper at all this week."

"Well, I have someplace special we have to get to," he explained. "We have to go."

"Go where?" I asked.

"To the mall."

"We're going to the mall?" I asked in disbelief. "You hate the mall."

"I hate shopping, and we're not going to the mall to do any shopping."

"Why else would you go to the mall except to shop?" Kia asked.

"You'll find out when we get there."

"You're not going to tell us?" I asked.

He shook his head. "It will make the surprise even better. Come on."

We spun around and followed my father out to his car.

"What about supper?" I asked. "What about mom? Is she coming?"

"We're going to eat at the mall, and your mom is really happy not to be coming with us. She's going to stay at home. She has some work to finish up."

"I guess it's too much to expect that both of you wouldn't be working at the same time," I said.

"Two weeks from now we'll all be not working for three weeks in a row when we're on holidays."

I was looking forward to us all being on holidays, but it would be hard not to have Kia around.

We climbed into the car.

"So will you at least give us a hint as to why we're going to the mall?" I asked. I didn't like surprises. I didn't like not knowing. It made me nervous.

"No hints. We'll be there in a few minutes."

My dad not giving a hint made me even more uneasy.

Before long we pulled into the mall parking lot. It seemed to be more crowded than usual. There were no spots up close except for the handicapped spaces. We cruised slowly down the lane until we finally found a few open spots at the very end of the lot.

"Seems like we're not the only ones here tonight," Kia said.

"Must be some sort of sale or something," I said.

"Maybe," my father agreed. "Then again, they could be here for the same reason as us."

"And that reason is?" I asked.

My father closed his car door and crooked his finger. "Come on."

There was a crowd of kids at the front doors— a whole pack of them off to the side, smoking. Smoking had to be the stupidest thing I could think of—I wondered if those three jerks from the rec center smoked. They seemed like the sort of people who would.

Kia made a loud fake coughing sound and gave the smokers a dirty look as we passed by, and they gave us a dirty look in return. She always did that.

She hated smoking as much as I did and didn't think it was fair that she had to inhale their stinky fumes. I was glad my father was with us in case they wanted to give us more than just a dirty look.

Inside, the mall was as crowded as the parking lot. People were milling around everywhere and there was loud music coming out of the overhead PA system. We threaded our way through the people until we reached the food court in the center of the mall. The tables had all been pushed back to the side and there was a stage set up. In front of the stage, a whole mass of people had gathered.

"Why don't you two work your way up to the stage, and I'll be right over there," my father said, pointing at the escalator.

"I still want to know what we—"

"Look! Look!" Kia exclaimed. "Look at the stage!"

The stage was empty except for some sound equipment and a microphone and...there was a big sign stretched above the stage. It read THE JYD PROJECT in gigantic white letters on an orange banner.

"JYD...like Junk Yard Dog...like Jerome Williams?" I gasped.

"The one and only," my father said.

"He's like one of my favorite players in the whole world!" I exclaimed.

"I know that. That's why I brought you here," my father said. "He's going to be here."

"Thank you so much … This is going to be fantastic!" I exclaimed.

"How did you know he was going to be here?" Kia asked.

"I heard about it on the radio," my dad answered. "Junk Yard Dog, along with his brother Johnnie and a motivational rapper—I think his name is Q something—have created a special project. They go out to hundreds of schools to speak to kids."

"This is a mall," I said, pointing out the obvious.

"They go out wherever there are people, young and old, to hear their message."

"You know a lot about them," Kia said to my father.

"I checked out their website—www.JYDproject. org—after I heard they were coming to town and were going to be here today. You two should go up closer to where the action is going to take place. I'll be right over here."

Kia and I started snaking forward through the crowd. It was pretty full, but there was enough space for us to move forward until we were only four or five rows from the stage.

All of a sudden the music got louder and louder, the bass pounding. It continued to swell even louder, and there were lights flashing. Then it stopped.

"Ladies and gentlemen, boys and girls, the JYD Project presents the Mission Possible Tour!" a voice yelled over the PA system.

People started to cheer as a young man bounded out onto the stage, microphone in hand. He had a big smile on his face as he bounced across the stage.

"Good afternoon, everybody!" he called out. "It is so good to be here with you. Are you all happy to be alive today?"

The crowd roared back its approval.

"I can't hear you!" he called out.

The crowd—including Kia and me—screamed even louder.

"My name is Steve Coleman, but I'm known as QTMC That stands for Quest to Make Change. That is the mission of the JYD Project. To make change through words of encouragement and positive music. I'd like you all now to do something with me. I want you to lift up an arm—no, lift up *two* arms."

Kia raised her arms. I felt a little bit uncomfortable, but looking around the crowd I could see an ocean of arms stretching up all around us.

"I want to share a song with you," QTMC called out.

The music got louder, the beat stronger.

"One … two … one … two … let's do this!" He started rapping to the beat of the music, moving across the stage, waving his outstretched arms back and forth.

"Now, throw your hands in the air … throw your hands up in the air … keep them up in the air! If you're happy to be alive today say, 'Oh yeah!'"

"Oh yeah!" the audience yelled back and swayed along with him, hands held high, arms swaying back and forth. You couldn't help but move along with the beat as QTMC kept rapping.

I leaned closer to Kia. "This guy is really good," I yelled over the music.

"Fantastic!" she said back.

Kia wasn't just swinging her arms. She was swaying back and forth in time with the beat. She was really into the music that QTMC was performing. Looking around I could see that she wasn't the only one. All the people in the crowd looked like they were feeling the same way.

The song came to an end and the audience cheered and clapped and screamed.

"Thank you! Thank you all!" QTMC called out. "I'd like to introduce you to a special friend of mine ... a man who invited me to be part of the JYD Project ... to be part of this Triple Threat team. He's a man who speaks from the heart to thousands and thousands of students every year about setting goals, embracing education, investing in themselves and reaching for their personal best in everything. Can we all give it up for Mr. Johnnie Williams the Third!"

People started cheering. From the side of the stage came a second man. He was taller than the first. He had a beaming smile as he glided across the stage. He and QTMC shook hands and then did a body bump as music began playing in the background again.

"How are you all doing today?" he called out, and the audience yelled back a greeting.

"I'm so happy and grateful to be here today. My name is Johnnie Williams the Third. I'm here today to pass on a message of hope—a message that's important to me, to my good friend QTMC and to my brother ... you all know my little brother ... Jerome "Junk Yard Dog" Williams."

There was a cheer from the audience.

"My brother and I decided that it was important for us to give back to our community. We created the JYD Project, a five-year plan to motivate 500,000 students. The JYD Project offers seven community outreach programs. Our programs aim to inspire youth to excel in academics and develop their self-confidence. I believe that the majority of our society's problems are man-made, leaving the power of solving them in our hands. I'm here today to tell you that the mission is possible.

"We all face challenges, we all have things that go wrong or go different than the way we'd hoped. You know you only have one life to live. Does anybody know what is the most precious thing you possess?"

People put up their hands or yelled out answers—cars, a house, money.

Johnnie Williams shook his head. "The most precious thing you have is time. You can lose a house or a car and you can get it back. You can lose all your money and you can get it back. But time ... once it's gone, it's gone. It will never come back. That means you can't waste your time. It's too important.

"Now, at this time, I want to introduce you to somebody special...somebody who set many goals and reached those goals. I often say he's my little brother. I can't really say that anymore because he's bigger than me...but he's still one of my younger brothers. Let's put our hands together and welcome my brother...Jerome, Junk Yard Dog!"

Everybody screamed and yelled as JYD bounded onto the stage. There was a huge smile splitting his face and he wore sweats and his trademark red headband. He shook hands with, and hugged, his brother and then QTMC. Johnnie Williams had looked tall until he stood there with JYD—he was big, really big.

"Hello, everybody. I am so pleased to be here today to speak to all of you. You make me feel so welcome the way you cheer and call out."

Behind me a couple of kids started to bark.

"Did I hear barking?" JYD called out. "Did I?"

A whole bunch of kids, including Kia, started to bark like a pack of dogs.

"Can you bark for us, JYD?" somebody yelled from the crowd.

"You know it! BARK! BARK! BARK!" he called out in a deep, deep voice. The crowd started cheering again.

"I have a question. Can anybody out there tell me what JYD stands for?"

"Junk Yard Dog!" a hundred voices yelled back.

"You're right, it does stand for Junk Yard Dog on the court because I do a little bit of growling when I'm out there. I go chasing that ball like a big old dog trying to get his favorite toy. But JYD also stands for something else when I'm not on the court. I'm going to tell you and I want you to call it out back to me when I tell you. You ready?"

"We're ready!" Kia yelled.

"The J means "Just be yourself.' Everybody repeat, J means ... "

"Just be yourself!" people repeated.

"That's good. The Y stands for "You have to set some goals.' So Y means ... "

"You have to set some goals!" the crowd screamed.

"Excellent. And the D simply means "Do your best.' So D is for ... "

"Do your best!" the entire crowd shouted.

"That's it! Just be yourself. You have to set some goals, and always do your best."

The crowd began cheering and the music, which was playing quietly in the background, got louder and louder and louder.

QTMC came forward, microphone in one hand, and he and JYD did a high five.

"This song is something special!" QTMC called out. "It's called the JYD song ... and if you know the words, you can rap along with me. Here it goes!"

The music got louder and then background singers began singing exactly what JYD had told us—Just be yourself, You have to set some goals, Do your best, JYD.

"No one can take away your education ... If your dream gets blocked, what can you fall back on?" QTMC rapped.

"Isn't that what your mother said to you today?" Kia asked.

I shot her a dirty look.

"Next time I'll tell her she should put it in a rap," Kia kidded.

I leaned close to Kia. "How about you just shut up and listen to the man."

QTMC kept on rapping, and when the song ended, the crowd cheered out its approval.

"You know, I'm going to be humming that song for the rest of the day," Kia said.

"Like I said, just shut up."

Johnnie and JYD came back up to the front of the stage as the cheering died down.

"I hope you're hearing QTMC's words with your ears and your heart," Johnnie said. "Now we need ourselves a volunteer!"

Hundreds of people raised their hands and voices.

"How about that young lady right there," JYD said, and to my shock he was pointing at Kia!

She practically jumped up into the air and then made her way through the crowd, up the steps and onto the stage. She shook hands with Johnnie and JYD. Kia looked tiny beside them.

"What's your name?" Johnnie asked.

"Kia."

"What a pretty name. I'm going to have Kia and my brother demonstrate something very important."

QTMC tossed Johnnie a basketball.

"When we were growing up, my father and my mother taught us a lot of things about life and about basketball. One day my father took us out to the court and handed me a basketball."

Johnnie handed the ball to Kia.

"He taught us about something called the triple threat. Does anybody know what the triple threat is?"

"I know!" Kia squealed.

"You do? Tell us then," Johnnie said.

"Triple threat means you can do three things with the basketball," Kia said. "You can shoot the ball or you can dribble or you can pass."

"Excellent!" Johnnie said, and JYD gave her a high five. Actually it was a high five for Kia and a sort of medium five for him.

"The first thing you can do is shoot. Go ahead, Kia, pretend you're going to shoot for a basket behind my brother."

Kia held the ball up like she was going to shoot. Suddenly JYD put his arms up and moved right in front of her. He was practically blocking the sky! He reached forward and put one hand on the ball so there was no way Kia was going to be able to shoot.

"Can't shoot, so what do you do now?" Johnnie asked.

"Dribble." Kia began dribbling the ball, moving away from JYD. She did a little crossover move, feeding the ball through her legs, and the crowd roared its approval.

51

"This girl's got game!" JYD called out, and the crowd cheered even louder.

Part of me wished it was me up there dribbling the ball. Part was happy for Kia and just plain glad it wasn't me up there in front of everybody.

"And now what are you going to do?" Johnnie asked as he, JYD and even QTMC closed in on Kia from all sides.

"I'm going to pass!" she yelled.

The ball came rocketing out into the audience, directly at me! I put my hands up just in time to catch the ball before it smashed me in the nose.

Kia raced across the stage, away from the triple coverage. Instinctively I threw the ball back to her.

"Let's have a big hand for our volunteer, Kia!" Johnnie called out as the audience applauded.

JYD motioned for Kia to toss him the ball. He caught it, pulled out a marker and started writing—he was autographing it ... that had to mean ... He tossed the ball back to Kia. She'd gotten an autographed ball! Now I really wished I had been up there!

Kia came back through the audience, accepting congratulations as she passed.

"What did he write?" I asked.

She shrugged. "I haven't looked."

I turned the ball over. It read: "Kia, you're a triple threat ... JYD, #13."

"You're so lucky," I said.

"You want it?"

"Me? You want to give me your personally signed ball?"

"Sure. It'll make up for the one that got destroyed."

"I can't take your ball," I said as I tried to press it back into her hands.

"Why not?"

"For one thing, it's yours. Second, it's even got your name on it. You keep it ... you deserve it for having the guts to go up there on the stage."

"I guess you're right. Afterwards we'll get him to sign something for you too."

"A triple threat isn't only for basketball," Johnnie Williams said. "Having options is what you need to get through life. Growing up, I thought I was going to be a professional basketball player. One day as I was playing for the school team, a terrible thing happened. I was going up for a dunk, and as I soared up, the man I was trying to beat ducked down. I went up and over, head over heels, landing on my arm. I shattered my elbow. And that ended my career as a ball player."

"You always need options," JYD said. "My brother kept his head up. He looked at his options, then adjusted his triple threat. And the option he pursued was what our parents always said. Get an education. And an education isn't something that just happens in school. It can happen every day ... every time you pick up a book, you gain knowledge. You learn new things that will help you succeed.

"You have to read to succeed," JYD continued. "Nobody can ever take that away from you, not ever. Every time you read, you gain something that nobody can ever take away from you. Knowledge helps you rise to the top."

"JYD is right." Johnnie added. "And there were lots of people who supported him, who helped him rise to the top to become the person and the player he is today."

"I want to tell all my fans in the dog pound to keep your heads up and rise to the top. Because all your support has helped me rise, and now my goal is to help you all rise!" JYD said.

"And that sounds like a cue for everyone to point toward your dreams!" Johnnie yelled out.

QTMC came back onto the stage as the music soared. A pounding beat. Everywhere in the audience, people raised their hands, as JYD and Johnnie were doing on the stage.

"Come on, rise to the top!" QTMC rapped. "Keep rising, growing from boys to men, from girls to women!"

Kia started dancing on the spot, deliberately bumping her hip against me again and again, almost forcing me to move along with her and the music.

As the music faded, the crowd applauded once more. QTMC took a bow, and JYD and Johnnie came forward.

"We want all of you to join us now…join us in our mission," Johnnie said. "A mission to encourage youth to shoot for their dreams, to dribble around obstacles and to pass on your support to others."

"And that mission is possible," JYD said.

"You want to be a carpenter or a lawyer, a teacher, a police officer, or run your own business you can do it."

"The mission is possible," JYD repeated.

"Starting today. Focus on your goals. Think of ways to obtain the things you need. Give back to the community. Chill along the journey to enjoy the moments," Johnnie said.

"Because the mission is possible."

In the background the music started up again. A beautiful, high-pitched woman's voice started singing over and over again, "The mission is possible!"

"Thank you all for coming today!" Johnnie yelled out to the crowd.

The music surged louder and Johnnie and JYD moved along the whole front of the stage, reaching down, giving hand slaps and handshakes, waving and smiling. They then turned, bowed and left the stage to a final roar of applause.

5

"This is one long lineup," Kia said.

We'd been in line for over thirty minutes. We'd already had our program, and Kia's ball, signed by both Johnnie and QTMC.

"I can't believe how long it's taking," I said.

"We can just go," Kia said. "I've already got JYD's autograph."

"I want to get it too."

"It's a strange concept, all of these people standing here so that they can get some guy to sign his name on a piece of paper."

"First off, I don't want him to sign a piece of paper," I said, holding up the basketball that my father had just bought for me. "And second, he isn't 'some guy'—he's Jerome Williams, the Junk Yard Dog."

"I know who he is. He's an NBA basketball player."

"My favorite player."

"I know he's your favorite. I've just never really understood why he's your favorite," Kia said.

"He's a great player."

"There are lots of great players in the NBA. Why is he your favorite?"

"I just like the way he plays. He plays with heart."

"I'll give you that much."

"I even remember when he became my favorite player. It was a game about a year ago. He didn't start the game. He came in off the bench in the second quarter, but he still got four steals, fourteen boards and twelve points."

"A double-double. Those are good stats."

"But more than the stats was the way he played. His first steal he knocked the ball away and then went sliding across the floor, knocking people down, to get the loose ball. He was up and down that court, spinning, jumping, grabbing boards, defending his man. And the whole time he's smiling, looking like he's just having fun."

"He does smile a lot," Kia agreed. "And I've got to admit that I like the way he plays too. He plays like he's bigger than he is."

I chuckled. "Isn't it strange that somebody who stands six feet nine inches tall isn't considered that big?"

"That's the NBA. I wonder what it was like growing up being that tall. I bet people would always be staring at you and making stupid comments and stuff."

"Maybe. You could ask him," I suggested. "We're almost there."

There were no more than a dozen people in front of us. I watched as JYD signed another slip of paper. He was smiling and joking with the little girl and her mother. He didn't seem to be in any rush and actually looked like he was enjoying himself—the way he seemed to do when he was playing ball.

Kia and I had collected autographs from different players. The best time was after a game. When we went down to see the Raptors play at the Air Canada Center, there was a place where you could go after the game and ask for autographs. Most of the players were pretty good and would sign things. They'd joke around, pose for pictures, and one even gave Kia his headband—she practically had to wring it out, it was so soaked with sweat.

A couple—not many, but a couple—had been jerks, just ignoring us. One even muttered under his breath and then said something about how we were just going to sell it, so he wasn't going to give us his autograph.

I knew that if I ever made it that far, there was no way in the world I'd ever brush somebody off—especially a kid. I'd treat them well. The way JYD was treating people today.

As we got closer, I could make out little bits of conversation. JYD suddenly burst into laughter, a big, booming, friendly laugh that was quickly joined by the people he was talking to. He reached out and signed the little boy's shirt. He then shook hands with both the boy and his mother and said goodbye.

"This is an awfully long wait," Kia said.

"Keep your voice down," I said to Kia. "He might hear you."

"So what? It's not like I'm saying anything bad."

"It's just that if we can hear him, he can hear us," I explained.

"And?"

"Just keep your voice down ... please."

We continued to inch forward until we were next

in line. He was joking with the people in front of us, a smile on his face. He finished signing their papers, said goodbye, and they moved on. We were next.

"Kia, it's good to see you!" he exclaimed. "I'm glad you stayed around."

"I wanted to get an autograph for my friend. This is Nick."

"Pleased to meet you, Nick. How're you doing?"

He reached out and shook my hand. It basically disappeared inside his huge mitt. His hands were enormous, but his handshake was gentle.

"I'm pleased to meet you, Mr. Williams, sir."

"You don't have to call me Mr. Williams or sir. JYD will do just fine."

"Okay, sure, Mr. JYD."

He laughed. "Just plain JYD, but obviously your parents raised you to be polite."

I felt a bit strange. I knew what his voice sounded like because I'd heard him in line and in interviews, but now he was talking to me.

"Are you two brother and sister?" JYD asked.

"No, best friends," Kia said.

"You two ever get hassled about being best friends?"

"Sometimes," I admitted.

"They say stupid things, like asking us if we're boy-friend and girlfriend or saying we talk like an old married couple."

"Don't let 'em give you any grief. You keep hanging out with your best bud."

"Could I ask you a question?" Kia asked.

"Shoot."

"When you were growing up, did people ever give you a hard time about being so tall?" Kia asked.

"I wasn't that tall," JYD said.

"Come on, seriously," Kia said.

"Seriously. When I graduated from high school I was only about six feet tall. I did my growing when I was in college. I grew nine inches."

"Wow!" I gasped.

Kia looked at me. "Still hope for you to become a center."

JYD chuckled. "So you two play some ball."

"We play a lot of basketball," Kia replied.

"Looks like you're pretty good."

"Not good. Great!" Kia replied.

This time JYD burst into laughter, and I couldn't help laughing along—his laughter was infectious.

"Nothing like being confident," he said.

"No, we really do play pretty well," I said. "We've been playing on the same rep team for years."

"And last summer our three-on-three team won the city Hoop It Up contest," Kia added.

"Excellent! Then you must play some great ball. You know, playing ball is one of the two best things you can do. You know what the other is, right?"

"Reading," I said.

He smiled. "Good to know the message got through. Do you read much?"

"Every day for twenty minutes," I said, not explaining that it wasn't my idea.

"What are you reading right now?" JYD asked.

"I'm reading a novel by Matt Christopher."

"He's a good writer," JYD said. "When you're reading one of his books, it feels like you're practically watching the game he's describing."

"Yeah, exactly," I said.

"Now, I've already signed the ball Kia has. Do you want me to sign that shiny new basketball?" he asked.

He took my ball. It seemed so little in his hand. It looked like he could palm it with one finger and his thumb.

"That's a fine-looking basketball," he said.

"My father bought it so I could get it signed. He

would have bought Kia one as well if you hadn't given her the ball."

"Sounds like you got yourself a good father."

"He's the best."

JYD's smile grew. "That's so nice you feel that way. Family's so important."

He put the tip of his pen to the ball. In big bold letters he wrote: "Nick, keep reading and keep playing! JYD."

"So you told that to your father lately?" JYD asked.

"Told him what?"

"That you think he's the best."

"Um ... not really ... I guess."

"Never put off saying or doing the right thing. Tell him today, okay?"

I nodded. "I'll tell him."

"It's a shame, though, that he bought you a bad ball," JYD said.

"What do you mean? It looks like a good ball."

"What good is a basketball that can't bounce?"

He handed me back the ball. It was soft because it hadn't been filled up.

"I just have to pump it up and it will be fine," I said.

"I see. So to make the ball work you have to have something inside of it."

"Um … yeah … air."

"That's right, it has to be inflated. For your mind to work, you have to have something inside of it too. That's what reading does. It inflates your mind." He paused. "I want you to take good care of this," he said, touching a finger against the side of my head. "And this," he said, tapping the ball. "Keep them both inflated."

"I'll make sure."

"Hopefully better than he did with the last signed ball," Kia said.

I shot her a dirty look.

"You had a problem with another signed ball?" JYD asked.

I pulled the ball in close to my chest, to show that I'd protect it, but also because I was afraid he might take it away from me.

"It got run over by a bus," I said quietly.

"A bus? What was a bus doing on a basketball court?"

"The bus was on a road," I answered.

"So what was your ball doing on a road?" JYD asked.

"That's where it ended up when this jerk kicked it over the fence of the court and—" Kia answered.

"But I'll treat this one a lot better," I said, cutting her off. I felt stupid and embarrassed about the whole thing and really didn't want to talk about it. "Besides, there's lots of other people in line still ... JYD doesn't have time to hear this story."

"I have as much time as you have story," JYD said. He turned to face the next people in line. "I'll get to everybody. I hope you don't mind if I hear the rest of this story, do you?"

"Not at all," the man said. "Besides I want to know why some jerk would kick a kid's ball over a fence, too."

JYD turned back to us. "So what happened?"

"We were going to the rec center," Kia said.

"Really we were just going for a swim," I said. "But there's a basketball court there."

"A really nice court," Kia added. "So Nick brought along his basketball in his backpack."

"I always like to have a ball with me," I explained. "You never know when a game might happen."

"Sounds smart. Sort of like being a Boy Scout, always be prepared."

"So the court was open, there was nobody on it," Kia continued.

"It was the middle of the afternoon, and I think

it was too hot for people to play. So we just started playing when these guys came over."

"Big guys," Kia said. "Like teenagers or even older. They were really big...not big like you, but a lot bigger than us."

"And one of these guys—these *big* guys—kicked your ball over the fence?" JYD asked.

"The biggest one," Kia answered. "And he told us that it was his court and that we couldn't play there. He told us that if we ever came back, it wouldn't just be the ball that he kicked over the fence."

"I hate bullies," JYD said. "I guess we've all had bullies pick on us."

"You've been picked on?" I asked.

"No matter how big you are, there's always somebody bigger or badder who gets his kicks picking on people. Can't understand why somebody thinks it makes them a man to pick on somebody smaller than them."

"That's what we said, too," Kia said.

"I just wish there was something I could do to make it better," JYD said.

"Signing the ball helped. Listening to you and your brother and QTMC today helped."

68

"That's what we're here for. Just curious, since this happened, have you gone back?" JYD asked.

"It just happened today."

"Today. Must still sting bad. You planning on going back?"

"We'd like to go back and beat them at basketball," Kia said. "They told us we could come back when we were able to beat them in a game of three-on-three and..."

Kia stopped talking, but the look on her face meant that she hadn't stopped thinking. What could she possibly have in mind? Oh, no...she couldn't! Not even Kia had enough nerve to do that.

"You know, JYD, you said you wished there was something you could do to help."

"Kia, don't!" I exclaimed.

"I'm just going to ask. It couldn't hurt to ask."

"Go ahead, shoot, what do you want to ask me?"

"Well...I was sort of wondering if you would play some basketball with us?"

6

We stood off to the side, watching the court from a safe distance. We could see them playing—as clear as day—but they couldn't see us that well. They were out there, the three big goons. We'd been watching for almost thirty minutes and had seen them play against two other teams. They'd won both games. Easily. Maybe they were jerks, but they did know how to play ball. They clearly were the best players in the park. That made the whole thing even stupider... more stupid. Did we really think that we had a chance in the world of beating these guys... even with JYD as the third member of our team?

I shook my head. Only Kia would ever think of asking JYD to play ball with us. Okay, sure, I'd thought of it too—once I saw where she was going.

But nobody except Kia would ever have enough nerve to actually ask him to play.

When Kia popped the question, I wanted to just scurry away. I felt so embarrassed. And then JYD asked some more questions and—to my complete shock—he said that he'd do it. I just couldn't believe my ears. Jerome "Junk Yard Dog" Williams was going to be joining Kia and me in playing a game of three-on-three. Unbelievable, simply unbelievable. So here we were, standing in the trees, waiting for JYD to drive up so that we could play a game of three-on-three against the three stooges.

Then came the hard part. We told my dad and then my mom and Kia's parents about JYD coming to the park to play basketball with us. They were all excited and happy. The big problem was that we didn't tell them why he was coming—just that he was going to be in the area and he said he liked to play street ball. My father talked about what an incredible experience that would be—to play ball with a genuine NBA player...a dream come true. He was right. It was like a dream...a dream I hoped wouldn't become a nightmare.

Of course our parents wanted to come and watch—who could blame them? We told them that he was showing up at two o'clock and that we were going early to "warm up." Actually everything was supposed to start just after one.

I hated lying, but we couldn't very well tell them the truth—that would involve way too much explaining and they might say no or get mad at us for not telling them what happened in the first place.

Thank goodness we told the story to my father first and then he told everybody else. My mother would have figured things out if I'd told her. Maybe it was her training as a reporter or something, but she was really good at seeing through things.

Kia and I had come up with a plan. We needed to challenge them to a game before JYD arrived so they wouldn't have a chance to see him and back out. If things worked out, we could play them, win, and they'd leave before our parents got there. Then all they'd see is what we told them—JYD fooling around on a court with us.

"What time is it?" Kia asked.

"Two minutes later than the last time you asked, which makes it ten minutes to one."

"He'll be here soon."

"If he's coming," I said.

"Why wouldn't he be coming?" Kia asked.

"Well … you know."

"Know what?"

"It's just that he's a big star. He's got lots of places he should be, lots of things he should be doing."

"And he told us that this was the place he was going to be and the thing he was going to be doing," Kia said. "You were there when he agreed."

"I know. I heard him … it's just … "

"Just what?"

"It's just that maybe he didn't think he had any choice but to say yes. Maybe he thought it over and then he realized that he couldn't make it."

"No, he wouldn't do that … would he?" she asked.

I thought about what he'd said, what I'd read about JYD, the things he and Johnnie and QTMC had said at the performance, the person I thought he was.

"No," I said, shaking my head. "JYD gave his word and he's going to be here," I said.

"You're sure, right?"

"I'm sure."

"Well, in that case, it's time. Come on."

Kia stood up and started walking toward the court. I got up and trailed after her. For better or worse we were going to do it. We walked through the gate and onto the edge of the court. At first nobody noticed. They were all looking at the action on the court and not two little kids standing at the side.

Standing there, watching, I started to get more nervous again. What were they going to say when they saw us? How would they react? I knew JYD would come if he could, but things did happen. What if he got caught in traffic or slept in? What if he slept in and he came but was thirty minutes late? Thirty minutes when these big guys could kick our ball—and us—over the fence.

Kia started dribbling her ball. She was using the ball that JYD had signed yesterday. My ball was safely at home. One ball drop-kicked over the fence was enough.

"Hey!" Kia yelled and I practically jumped out of my shoes. "We get the winners!"

The guy dribbling the ball stopped. Everybody stopped. The people standing and watching the game all turned to look at us. That was smart. Whatever was going to happen to us was going to be a lot more interesting than what was happening in the game.

"What are you two doing back here?" the biggest of the jerks asked.

"Taking you up on your invitation," Kia said. "You told us that if we wanted to come back we had to play, so we're here to play you."

Everybody started to laugh. I couldn't blame them. This was a joke. Me and Kia playing them.

"Go away, kids," the biggest guy said.

"You said to come back when we were ready to play, so we're back. We challenge you three to a game. That is unless you're afraid to play us," Kia added, and the laughter got even louder.

"You two have got to be either the bravest little midgets I ever met or the stupidest."

"Could be both," I said, to another rain of laughter. Actually I wasn't joking. This was an act of stupidity as much as bravery.

"Either way, as soon as you finish with your game, we get to play the winners," Kia said.

"Like you said the last time, there's only two of you, so a three-on-three game would be hard … unless you're giving us a handicap … you know, letting us outnumber you like this," he said.

"You got a big enough handicap as it is," Kia said. "You know, the way you can't drive to your left-hand side if your life depended on it."

There was more laughter and applause. Not that

he'd driven much—mostly he just set up down on low post and powered through his coverage—but we'd noticed his difficulties when we were watching them play. Right or wrong, though, it wasn't the smartest thing to say to somebody as big and mean as him.

He walked right over to us. As he got closer I got more anxious. I had to fight the urge to simply grab Kia, turn and run away as fast as my legs would carry me. I stood still. He stopped when he was right in front of us—actually he was towering above us. His shirt was stuck against his body, held in place by the same sweat that dripped off his face.

He bent down so that his face was practically level with mine.

"Whether I drive with my left hand or not, it isn't my life that's in danger here," he said softly.

I swallowed hard.

"You scared?" he asked.

"Yeah," I admitted honestly.

"I'm not!" Kia snapped.

"Maybe you should be," he said.

"What are you going to do, kick this ball over the fence too?" Kia asked, holding the ball out.

I couldn't believe her nerve. She had to be the gutsiest person I'd ever met. She probably really *wasn't* afraid of him.

He shook his head. "Nope. Shouldn't have done that to your ball," he said, pointing at me. "Tell you what. You two amuse me. A couple of gutsy little dudes."

"Do I look like a dude to you?" Kia demanded.

"Okay, okay, don't get mad!" he said, holding his hands up like he was surrendering. "You want to stand around and watch, you can, and nobody will bother you."

"We don't want to stand around and watch," Kia said. "We want to play ... against you and your buddies. That is unless you lose the game you're playing and then we'll play the other team instead. It doesn't matter to us who we beat as long as we get a chance to beat somebody."

He turned to his two buddies. "She's got guts, don't she?" He turned back to us. "Again, little girl, no matter how much you want to play us in three-on-three, you're still short a player."

"He'll be here ... soon."

The big guy shook his head, but he smiled.

"Come on, Ben, let's play ball!" one of his partners yelled out.

"Coming ... coming!" he called out. "Your third man comes, we'll play you. I figure that's the only way I'm ever going to get you to shut up."

That probably wouldn't get Kia to shut up either.

"Just one more thing," Kia said. "I want to make sure you remember what you said. If we beat you, you'll go away and leave the court, right?"

"If you beat us, I'm not just leaving the court. I'm leaving the planet!" one of the others said to a whole chorus of laughter.

"So you'll go away?" Kia asked.

"We'll go ... Of course, that means when we win, we'll never see you two again ... right?"

"If you win, then we'll go," Kia said. "Deal?"

"Deal."

Kia held out her hand and the big guy shook it.

"Now if you don't mind, how about letting us get back to this game ... you know, so we can figure out who gets the honor of playing against you next game."

"No problem," Kia said.

We walked off the court and stood over by the fence.

"What time is it?" Kia asked.

I looked at my watch. "He was supposed to be here two minutes ago."

"Nick," Kia said quietly. "Is that him?"

"Where?"

She pointed to a black Escalade that was pulling into the parking lot. It had fancy rims and was big and shiny. I couldn't see anybody through the tinted windows. It slowed down and the passenger window glided open. It was JYD! Kia waved and he smiled and gave a little wave back.

"Hey!" Kia yelled out, and the players on the court turned around. "Our third player is here." She pointed to the SUV. "He's right there."

The guy looked in the direction she had pointed. He strained to see. "Where?"

The door of the SUV opened and JYD climbed out. He gave a little wave.

"That's ... that's ... "

"That's our third player," Kia said.

"But he's ... he's Junk Yard Dog Williams!"

"Yeah, he is. You said we could get anybody we wanted, so we did."

"But he's in the NBA."

"You said anybody," Kia replied. "If you didn't

want us to get anybody in the NBA, you should have mentioned it."

JYD's brother Johnnie and QTMC got out of the SUV as well. The three of them slowly sauntered through the gate and onto the court. They all looked big and serious and more than a little bit scary.

Then JYD flashed one of his huge smiles and the tension vanished.

"How's it going, everybody!" he called out, and everybody rushed forward, talking and holding out their hand for him to shake or a basketball for him to sign.

7

It took a long time for things to settle down. JYD had signed everything that everybody had wanted him to sign. He even signed things for the three stooges. I almost wished that he hadn't. After all, they were the enemy, the bullies we were here to beat. I wished he'd signed everybody's stuff except for theirs. Then again, he'd signed their basketballs. Maybe after the game I could kick one of those balls over the fence and see how they felt about it.

"These guys can play some ball," JYD said as we watched them finish up their game.

"They are pretty good," I agreed. "But you're a lot better ... right?"

"Of course he's better. These are just good high school players," Kia said, and I knew that she was right.

"Do you think we can take them?" I asked.

"That's not the most important thing," JYD said.

"It isn't?" Kia asked.

He shook his head.

"Then what is the most important thing?" I asked.

"Lots of other things. For example, it's important that you and Kia think we can take them." He paused. "Well, do you?"

"With you on our team we can't miss," Kia said. "I figure we'll just keep feeding you the ball and then you'll score."

"That could work," JYD agreed. "Just one problem with that plan. If I score all the points, what does that mean?"

"It probably means that we win," Kia said.

"We'd win the battle, but you two would lose the war."

"I'm confused," I said. "There's no war here ... at least I hope there isn't." I didn't want to get into a fight with these guys even if JYD was on our side.

"Let me explain," JYD said. "These guys probably know that I'm a better ball player than they are."

"If they don't, they're bigger idiots than even I thought," Kia said.

"Let's not do any name calling," JYD said.

"Sorry," Kia apologized.

"So win or lose this game, it isn't about how they feel about me and my game. It's how they feel about you that counts."

"They think we're a couple of little goofs … is it okay for me to call us names?"

JYD smiled. "It's better to not put down anybody, including yourself. Maybe they do think you're goofs. The big thing this game is going to do is make a difference in the way they see you two."

"It will make a difference if we win," Kia said. "They'll see us as being part of the team that won."

"Don't you want more than that?" he asked.

"What did you have in mind?" I asked nervously.

"You said you two were good players."

"No," Kia said. "I told you we were great players."

"Then maybe that's what you have to show them. You have to show them that you can play."

"We can try … but they're a lot older and bigger than us."

"They're bigger for sure. I play against bigger people all the time. It just means you have to play harder."

"We can play hard, but can we play hard enough to beat them?" I asked.

"I don't know," JYD said. "What I do know is that you're not here just to win the game."

"We're not?" Kia asked.

He shook his head. "You're here to win respect. If we win and I do all the scoring, the only one who's going to be respected is me. If we lose, but you two play your hearts out, then you're going to win something more important than a game." He paused. "You're going to earn respect. From them. From me. And from yourselves. That's more important than any game results."

"I guess that makes sense," I said. "But couldn't you score some of the points? A few maybe?"

"Maybe a few, but not many. So what's your game plan?"

"Our plan was that when we had the ball, we were going to give it to you and you'd score, and when they had the ball, you'd stop them," Kia said.

"We've ruled that plan out. Here's what I'm thinking. On defense we go with a two-one zone. You two chase the ball, staying up on the top of the key, trying to force them to come inside ... and that's where I'm going to be waiting, inside, right in the paint, under the net."

"To block shots and get boards," I said.

"That's the place to be."

"How about when we have the ball?" Kia asked.

"I figure at first they're going to be keying on me. I'll get at least double coverage, don't you think?" he asked.

"Sometimes triple coverage. They're not expecting anything from us," I said.

"And that's where we're going to surprise them," he said.

"Surprise them? We're even surprising us," Kia said.

"That element of surprise is going to work for us. They're not expecting you two to score, so they won't be covering you. You two have a favorite spot to shoot?" JYD asked.

"I like being underneath the net," I said. "I'm a power forward."

"I don't think that's going to work really well in this game," he said. "You have a place you like to spot up for a shot?"

"Either elbow."

"Good. That means the best way to open you up is with a pick and roll."

"You want me to pick for you?" I asked.

He shook his head. "These guys would run you down flat as a pancake. I was thinking I could pick for you. Send it in to me and then you drop back to the elbow whenever you see me drive and I'll kick the ball back to you."

"I can do that."

"Good. Kia, where's your spot?"

"I shoot pretty well from the three-point line by the baseline."

"Left or right side?"

"Both … either."

"Excellent. I want you to be running back and forth, setting up on both sides. You get open and we'll get you the ball."

"You get me the ball and I'll make my shots," Kia said confidently.

"You'll get the ball from both Nick and me. Nick, you're going to be point guard."

"I've never played point before."

"First time for everything. You have an advantage over these guys."

"I do?"

"Yeah. You're short."

"And just how is being short an advantage?" I questioned.

"It's an advantage when you're dribbling. You ever seen a seven-foot point guard?"

"I guess not."

"You never will. The point guards are always little guys...you know, maybe six feet six inches tops. Keep yourself low to the ground and watch out for them reaching in on you. Remember that for your shots as well. Both of you. You can't rush your rhythm, but they're going to get into your faces real fast to block or alter your shot. Get it away quickly or you'll be eating the ball."

"We'll get our shots away as quick as we can," I said.

"We have one other advantage going for us," JYD said.

"What's that?" I asked.

"I've been watching them while we've been talking. These guys got some game, but it's not a team game."

"What do you mean?"

"Everybody's trying to do things the hardest way possible. I get the feeling that they'd rather miss a fancy shot than make a simple one. Watch."

We turned to look at the game in progress. It was a close game. Both teams were good, although the three stooges were better. They scored another basket and somebody yelled out the score—they were up by five points.

It was also apparent that all six players were not only big, but good. There were a couple of good ball handlers on both sides, and the big guys were banging together under the net for the ball, pushing and shoving for position. There was no way I could compete with any of these guys—especially under the hoop. Rather than hoping for rebounds, I should be praying that nobody would kill me when they were taking the rebounds away from me.

As we continued to watch, it was clear that what JYD had said was true. There weren't two teams playing as much as there were two groups of three individuals. Easy passes were overlooked. Instead of passing to the open player, everybody was trying to beat his man off the dribble. Instead of looking for the high percentage shot, they were putting up off-balance, forced shots, some missing by a mile.

"These guys don't seem to know how to spell," JYD said.

"Spell? What do you mean?" Kia asked.

"They don't realize that there isn't an 'I' in team," JYD said. "The choices are to win as a team or lose as individuals."

Just as obvious as the way they were playing was the reason they were playing that way. It was hard to play when you only had one eye on the net. The other eye was looking at JYD. They were playing to impress rather than playing to win. I figured it would get even worse when he was actually out there on the court playing against them. That could only work for us too.

A long shot went up. The ball bounced hard against the backboard, slammed against the front of the rim, into the air, and then dropped in.

"That's game!" the big goof yelled.

JYD turned to me and Kia. "You two ready?"

"I was born ready," Kia said.

"Nick?"

I nodded my head. "I'm as ready as I'm going to be. Let's do it."

8

"Before we get started, we need to get properly introduced," JYD said. "I'm Jerome Williams, but you can all call me JYD."

"Pleased to meet you. I'm Ben," the big guy said as he pumped JYD's hand. He certainly didn't seem that big standing there beside JYD.

"And you've already met my teammates... although I don't know if you got names."

"Not really," Ben said, looking down at his shoes. He looked like he was embarrassed—and he should be embarrassed about the way he treated us.

"This here is my little brother, Nick."

"Your brother?" Ben asked.

"We're all brothers," JYD said.

Kia cleared her throat and JYD chuckled. "Of course, except for those of us who are sisters. This little lady is Kia."

"Yeah, I'm Kia."

Ben reached out his hand and for a split second I thought she was going to refuse to shake. Finally she offered her hand.

"I'm Devon ... I'm a big fan of yours," the second-biggest member of the team said. He had little baby dreads and a skimpy little mustache. He was tall—maybe six three—but he was also real thin. I actually wondered if I could box him out. Of course that was silly. Even if I held my position, he'd just reach up and over my head to get rebounds.

"Thanks, man. Pleased to meet you," JYD said as they shook.

Devon then offered his hand to Kia and then to me.

"I'm Ethan," the third player said and shook hands with all of us.

"I'm glad to be playing with all of you today. I'm sure we're going to have a good game."

"We're just thrilled to be playing with you ... this is a real honor," Ethan said.

"I'm honored that you'd let me play. Let's set some rules. Are we playing cutthroat or loser gets ball?"

"Whatever you want to play," Ben said.

"I like loser getting the ball. It makes for a more even game. What are the rules on turnovers or a change in possession?" JYD asked.

"The ball has to be taken outside the three-point line before you can score or the points count for the other team."

"Sounds fair. How many points to win?"

"First team to fifteen points. Anything inside the line is two, outside the three-point line counts for three."

"What about fouls?" JYD asked.

"You think you were fouled, you call it."

"Do you get shots?" JYD asked.

"No shots, just possession."

"Just possession…hmmmm…sounds like it almost pays to foul somebody. I guess that's okay if you're the biggest dog in the pound." JYD moved in real close to Ben. JYD wasn't smiling. He had a serious, scary look to him as he stared down at Ben. Ben backed off a half step.

"Course I expect a good clean game," JYD said. "Hard, but clean. I remember something my grand-father used to say to me. He said, Jerome, in my whole life I ain't never hit anybody…first."

Kia broke out laughing as JYD flashed a huge smile. I knew exactly what JYD was actually saying to these guys. Don't pick on the little kids or I'll pick on you. I just hoped that those three guys were smart enough to have figured it out as well.

"Who gets first ball?" Ben asked.

"How about if we shoot for ball?" Kia suggested.

"Sounds good."

"You first," Kia said. "You make it, it's your ball. You miss and it's ours."

"Maybe you should go first," he said, offering the ball to Kia.

"No thanks. I figure it might be the only ball you sink all game, so go for it."

Ben looked shocked and then angry as the fifteen guys standing around watching all laughed and jeered and cheered. They were dressed in sweats and basketball shoes, guys who had been playing or were ready to play.

We all walked over to the side as he took the ball and went to the foul line. He put up the shot. It clanked off the back rim and bounced off.

"Our ball!" Kia exclaimed as she rushed over and grabbed the ball before it could roll away.

Kia, JYD and I walked to the top of the key.

"Nick, put the ball in to me. Put it really high. Remember, I'm big and I can jump. Kia, you go down to your spot on the baseline. I'm going to fake a drive, kick it back out to Nick, and he's going to feed you. You put it up. Don't worry. Even if you miss, I'm getting the rebound."

"There isn't going to be a rebound to get," she said.

"That's the spirit." He held out his hand. "Hands in," he said.

I put my hand on top of JYD's, and Kia put her hand on top of mine. "Remember, if we try our best, we play as a team, we play with heart, then, no matter what the score, we walk away as winners. Okay, now break!"

I took the ball and walked over to the sideline. Ethan walked toward me but gave me lots of space. Both Ben and Devon covered JYD—one behind and one in front—as he set up at the top of the key. Kia was all by herself by the baseline.

"Check," I said as I bounced the ball to Ethan. He tossed it back.

JYD lifted up one of his arms. Ben and Devon reached up to try and cover him, but his arm extended well above their reach. If I tossed it high enough, they wouldn't be able to get it. But then again ... why would I even try?

"JYD!" I yelled and faked the pass to him.

Ethan jumped back, creating a triple team on JYD. I threw in a hard pass to Kia. She planted her foot, spun, aimed and threw up a shot. JYD fought his way through the other players, getting in position for the rebound in time to see the ball swoosh right through the hoop—nothing but net!

The small crowd at courtside exploded! People started whooping and hollering, and one guy ripped off his shirt and started waving it around his head! It was obvious whose side they were on. They probably didn't like being bullied by these guys any more than we did.

JYD patted Kia on the back. He then reached down and grabbed the ball. "I think this belongs to you," he said as he handed the ball to Ben. The other team had been so stunned that they hadn't even reacted to the shot or the basket.

"Smart," JYD said to me as I walked by. "You saw the open look and changed the play. That's the sort of thing a good point guard does."

Kia walked to the top and took the ball check while I scrambled over to cover Devon. Ethan threw it inbounds to Devon. It was a high, soft, lob pass that was a good three feet over my head. I couldn't have gotten it with a stepladder.

I backed over a few steps as Devon began dribbling. He was so smooth, feeding the ball back and forth through his legs, doing little stutter steps. He had great control of the ball. He broke left, and as I jumped over to cover, he crossed me over and turned the corner on me like I was a traffic pylon. Kia rushed off her man to try to help, but Devon beat her as well. He broke in, hit the paint and went to lay the ball in. JYD reached out and grabbed the ball, pinning it against the backboard.

Again the crowd just went wild! I stood there, stunned, as he dribbled out of the key and past the three-point line.

"Need some help!" he yelled out, and I unfroze and faded out and into the open.

He fired the ball at me. I caught it, but the force of the ball practically lifted me off my feet. I recovered and started dribbling. I expected somebody to rush me, but nobody came. Ben and Devon were all over JYD, and Ethan was fading off to the side, trying to stay close enough to Kia to get in her way if I put the ball to her.

Kia ran over to the far side and Ethan went with her. I had a lane to the net. I hesitated for a split second and then drove.

I was in the paint before Devon split off from his double coverage and came at me. I feathered a pass into the upraised arms of JYD. As everybody converged on him, I kept moving in and he sent the ball back to me for an uncontested, open layup. The ball bounced off the backboard and into the net!

For a third time the spectators cheered wildly, and Kia rushed over and gave me a high five.

"Now that was a power forward move off the give and go," JYD said. "We're gonna have to try that one again."

"That makes it five to nothing," Kia said. "You guys planning on scoring at all this game?"

JYD turned to her and motioned for her to come over. "No trash talk," he said quietly. "To get respect you have to give respect. Understand?"

"Sorry," Kia said. She went out to the top of the key as the ball came into play, once again coming to Devon.

He faked and juked and styled with the ball. He was good. It would have been even more impressive if somebody was covering him. He was out there, way beyond the three-point line, putting on a show.

Ben started yelling for the ball. He was at the top of the key, and Devon bounced in a pass to him. Instantly, JYD was right on his back. Ben started to back in, trying to power through JYD. Ben was big, but JYD was bigger. It was like watching a truck hit a brick wall. JYD stood his ground, finally reaching out and swatting the ball away.

I scrambled after it, but Ethan got there first, bouncing me off to the side, knocking me off my feet. I sprawled forward, my face plowing into the pavement.

"Time!" JYD yelled as he rushed over.

"It was an accident!" Ethan exclaimed.

"Loose ball foul!" Kia screamed.

JYD offered me a hand and pulled me to my feet.

"I'm okay," I said.

"I didn't mean to knock you over," Ethan said. "I'm really sorry, man." He offered me the ball.

I shook my head. "No foul ... it's still your ball. We were just both going for the ball," I said. "It wasn't your fault. You just got there first and got there bigger."

"You sure you're okay?" he asked.

"I'm fine. I've been hit harder before," I said, although never by anybody that big.

"Maybe we shouldn't even be doing this," Ethan said. "I don't want to hurt anybody. These two are just little. Maybe we should call the game."

"You call it now and we win," Kia said.

"I just don't want anybody getting hurt," Ethan said.

"Would it be better if we promise not to hurt you?" Kia asked. "Your ball. Let's get playing."

Ethan started dribbling. He threw a pass in to Ben, who once again tried to back JYD in. Ben was big—at least compared to Kia and me—but he was no match for JYD. Why didn't he see that?

JYD reached out and swatted the ball away again. Before either Kia or I could react, the ball bounced into Devon's hands. He put up a shot and it dropped for two.

"Nice shot," JYD said as he recovered the loose ball. He handed it to me. "I'll try to get open, but keep an eye open for Kia."

I stood up at the top of the court. Nobody came out to cover me. JYD was doubled, and Ethan was halfway between him and Kia.

Suddenly music came spilling across the court. QTMC was standing by the Escalade. The doors were wide open and he'd turned up the sound system so it was blasting out. It was one of the songs we'd heard yesterday. He bounded toward the crowd, his arms raised in the air, and the people watching all joined in.

It was then that I noticed it wasn't just those dozen or so guys anymore. There had to be three times that many people. There was a couple with a stroller, three guys sitting on their bikes, and what appeared to be a whole team of six- or seven-year-old soccer players, in uniforms, wearing cleats, standing by the fence. It looked like they'd abandoned their practice to watch the game. With the music blaring and everybody waving their hands in the air, it was starting to seem more like a concert than a basketball game.

"Come on, Nick, let's get playing!" Kia called out.

JYD broke toward me and away from the coverage. I tossed in a ball to his open arms. As they closed in on him, he pitched it out to Kia. Ethan rushed toward her, his arms raised to try to block the shot. She put it up, barely getting it over his outstretched fingers. The ball went way up, came down, hit the rim and bounced wildly away. JYD came out of nowhere, grabbed the ball out of the air and threw it down with a thunderous two-handed slam!

The crowd went crazy! People were screaming and yelling and running onto the court, slapping him on the back and just plain jumping around. He accepted a bunch of high fives and then shooed the people back onto the sidelines.

"Sorry about that," JYD said quietly to Kia and me. "I just couldn't resist."

"No need to apologize," Kia replied. "No need to resist. That was ... that was ... "

"Amazing," I said. "Just amazing."

The people kept on cheering. At that point I realized the crowd was getting bigger by the second. It looked like the whole rec center was emptying out—there was a stream of people coming toward the court. And there were cars ... lots of cars ... with more coming. The parking lot was filling up. I guessed word had gotten out that JYD was here, and people wanted to see him and find out what was going on. I knew that if I wasn't playing but had heard about it happening, I would have got here pretty fast. I did a quick scan of the crowd—thank goodness I didn't see any of our parents.

Once again Ethan inbounded the ball to Devon. Kia went out after Devon this time while I cheated over toward Ethan. Ben was underneath the basket, fighting for position against JYD. I watched him battle and lose as, each time he tried to secure his spot, JYD swam around him, arms and legs and body, and overwhelmed him. Ben kept fighting, though. I had to hand it to him. He wasn't giving up. Despite being outsized, outmuscled and out-skilled, he wasn't quitting.

Meanwhile, Devon was putting on a show for Kia, showing her the ball and drawing it back every time she reached out for it. Two things were obvious—he was good with the ball, and Kia didn't have a chance of getting it. He put on a move, breaking her off at the ankles, and drove around her. As JYD came out to cut him off, Devon sent the ball in to Ben. He had an easy lane to the net and laid the ball up and—JYD swooped out of nowhere, swatting the ball away! It went back to Ethan. He turned for the net, measured the shot and then put up a fifteen footer that dropped.

"You got yourself a really nice touch there, Ethan," JYD said as he came out and gave Ethan a pat on the back.

"Thanks," Ethan gushed.

JYD turned to Ben. "How old are you, son?"

"I'll be eighteen in September."

"I'm impressed. I didn't have your size or your footwork when I was your age. Hey, Johnnie!" JYD yelled over to his brother. "These boys can play some ball, can't they?"

"It's like Nick and Kia told you, these boys got game," Johnnie answered.

We walked out to the top of the key with the ball.

"Why are you being so nice to them?" Kia asked.

"I try to be nice to everybody. Being nice doesn't cost nothing. Besides, they *are* pretty good players."

"Yeah, but do we have to tell them?" she asked.

"What should we run now?" I asked, before Kia could stick her foot any deeper into her mouth.

"You're the point guard. You call the play."

"Okay...I...umm...want you to start at the top by me," I said to JYD. "You break for the net, arms raised, screaming for the ball. I'm going to fake an alley-oop pass to you. Kia, you swing from the left to the right side along the baseline. I'm going to put the ball in to you. Take the shot. If you miss, JYD is there for the board."

"You got it, chief," JYD said.

JYD stood right at the top. Ben and Devon were draped all over him.

"Break!" I yelled, and JYD fought through the two players.

"Nick!" he screamed and I faked a pass, drawing all three players to him.

Kia, uncovered and unobserved, spun around, completely open, hands up, waiting for the pass. I sent her the ball. It was slightly off the mark and she had to reach out to get it. Both Devon and Ethan rushed out toward her as Kia put the shot up. It was way long, clearing the net completely and landing right in JYD's outstretched hands. It looked more like a pass than a shot. He could easily put it back down and—he passed it out to me.

"Shoot!" JYD yelled.

I never shot from this far out—maybe this was the time to try.

"Put it up!"

I shot. It hit the rim and bounced away. JYD cleaned up the rebound again, tossing it right back to me. I hesitated for a split second and then put up another shot. This one was long—it hit the backboard and dropped in! The crowd roared out in reaction.

"That makes ten!" Kia yelled. "Ten to four."

As our opponents walked out to the top of the court to inbound the ball, I walked over to JYD.

"Why didn't you take the put back?" I asked.

"I'm not going to be taking any more shots."

"None?"

"Remember, it's about respect, not about winning. You two have earned some, now earn some more."

They brought the ball in and started to pass it around. It went from one player to another to the other and then back again. It seemed like they'd suddenly discovered passing. I guess what they'd really discovered was that JYD could only be in one place at a time. Actually, with his height and reach, he probably could be in two places at once, but he couldn't cover all three of them if they spaced themselves out.

Kia and I raced from player to player, chasing the ball, while JYD stayed in the paint to prevent anybody from driving. The problem was that even if we caught up to the ball, we couldn't get it. They just held it up, high over our heads, at a height that we simply couldn't get. They kept passing the ball, hoping that JYD was going to come out after them. He stayed planted under the hoop, and Kia and I kept chasing.

"Go ahead and take your time!" Kia yelled. "You only get one chance, and if you miss the shot, we own the rebound!"

She was right. We couldn't pressure the shot very much, but if it wasn't in the net, then JYD was going to scoop up the rebound, and there wasn't much they could do about that either.

The ball came out to Devon. He was set just outside the three-point line. He bounced the ball once, took aim and put up a shot. It was a high arching shot that dropped right through the hoop! The crowd cheered—although it wasn't nearly as loud as when we scored.

I took the ball out to the top and checked it with Ethan, who was practically standing on top of me. Ben was on JYD—but was there by himself. Devon was all over Kia. She ran, trying to get free, but he was just too tall and long and fast. That only left one choice. I put the ball in to JYD. He snared the high pass and I broke in. As I broke, I bumped into Ethan. Rather than abandoning me to double down on JYD, he was staying on me! I tried to get free, but it felt like being covered by a blanket. I couldn't get free enough for a return pass.

JYD started dribbling. He was smooth. He looked more like a guard than a power forward as he moved the ball back and forth, eluding Ben's feeble attempts to steal the ball. I knew JYD could easily beat him and drive for the net. I also knew he wasn't going to do it.

"Time out!" JYD yelled as he grabbed the ball.

Slowly we walked over to the fence where Johnnie and Steve were standing.

"Looks like they have it figured out," Johnnie said.

"I think so. It's going to get tougher from here on in, both on defense and offence."

"But we only need five more points," Kia said. "Two more shots—one from the three—and it's game."

"They're not going to let you get free for those shots. I'm just guessing, but I figure they probably think that if I score on them it's one thing, but if one of you score on them it's just embarrassing."

"Embarrassing?" Kia asked.

"Sure. How would you feel if you lost to a couple of five-year-olds?" JYD asked.

"Especially in front of all your friends and a gigantic audience," Johnnie added.

"I wouldn't like it," Kia said.

"And you'd probably do anything you could to avoid it. Expect things to get tougher ... and rougher."

"I'm not afraid," Kia said. "Bring it on."

"Anybody got any ideas?" JYD asked.

"We have to clear space, and the only way I can see doing that is by setting some picks," I said. "I'll send the ball in to you and we'll use you as a pick. That should open it up for one of us."

JYD set himself at the top of the key. Ben was on him, but JYD easily corralled my pass. Kia and I both broke toward him, trying to use JYD to peel off our man. We got there at about the same time, cut on both sides of him and—

"Switch!" Devon yelled, and suddenly Devon was covering Kia and Ethan was glued to my side. We were still covered, just by the other player. It hadn't worked at all.

I broke toward Kia. As she came toward me, I planted. She cut right by my screen and—

"Uggggg!"

I went flying backward as Devon plowed into me, the two of us tangling up as I smashed into the ground, Devon landing heavily on top of me. I struggled to turn around to see the action. Kia was free, driving the net. She put the ball up and the crowd roared as it dropped!

Devon pulled himself to his feet and offered me a hand. "You okay?" he asked.

I held up my arm. The whole elbow was scraped and raw. "Most of me."

"I could have really hurt you," Devon said.

I shrugged.

"You got guts, man."

"Thanks."

JYD walked over and took my arm, lifting it up to look at it. "Does it hurt much?"

"Not yet. Later ... but not as much if we win."

"When we win," Kia said, correcting me.

"I like that attitude, girl," JYD said. "Let's throw them a curve. Change the defense. Let's go man to man."

"What?" I asked in shock.

"Kia on the inbounds man, Nick on Ben and I'll take who's leftover."

"You want me to cover Ben?" I asked.

"I don't think he can beat you off the dribble. Keep your feet moving and hands up."

Ethan had the ball, and as we scrambled to cover our men it was obvious by the look on his face that he was shocked and surprised by our defense.

"Mismatch!" Ben yelled out.

So much for surprise. Ethan threw the ball in to Ben. Devon had faded way off to the side, drawing

JYD with him. I expected either JYD or Kia to double down on Ben, but neither did. They stayed outside with their men, leaving Ben and me, alone, at the top of the key. There was a smile on Ben's face. Obviously I wasn't the only one who'd noticed nobody was coming over to help.

"Keep your feet moving!" JYD called out.

"And remember he can't drive to his left!" Kia yelled. "He's useless to his left!"

Ben's smile was replaced by a scowl. He hadn't appreciated Kia's comments. I didn't appreciate them either. Getting him mad wasn't in my best interests.

Ben started dribbling. I knew this wasn't his strength. He was used having the ball passed to him once he was inside. He shifted over, the cross-over partially bouncing off his leg. If I hadn't been playing off, I might have got it...but there was no way I was going outside on him. Even more than not being a good ball handler, he wasn't an outside shooter. His whole game was inside and power. He hadn't attempted an outside shot during the whole time I'd watched him play. And even if he did have a shot, he'd have been nuts to take it. Why risk a lower percentage shot when he could stuff it in the net with a jam?

"Come on, Bennie!" somebody yelled from the sidelines. "Don't be afraid. The kid won't hurt you!"

There was a ripple of laughter from the crowd.

Ben scowled and his eyes almost glowed with anger. He lowered his head and drove the net. I shuffled over, blocking his lane, planting my feet and—he bowled into me, sending me backward into the air and then smashing down against the pavement!

"Charge!" Kia screamed.

The crowd roared, and when I looked over I saw a whole bunch of people put their hand behind their head—the signal for a charge.

"He was still moving!" Ben argued. "It was a block, not a charge!"

Devon walked over and took the ball from Ben's hands. "You're the only one here who saw it that way."

Devon offered me a hand and pulled me to my feet. My leg was as scraped up as my arm, and there was a tender spot on my side where some pointy part of Ben had slammed into my ribs.

"You okay?" Devon asked.

"If it's our ball, I'm good."

"Then you're good." He handed me the ball.

I walked it out to the top of the court. My leg was stinging badly and I was working at not limping.

"I'll put it in play," I said.

JYD leaned down. "Throw it in for the net," he whispered. "Give me an alley-oop."

"I thought you weren't going to score anymore," Kia said.

"I also thought it would be nice for you to live to see the end of the game. I can't just stand here and watch Nick get banged up. Send me the pass."

"Sure … if you're open."

JYD did a double take. His eyes widened and his mouth dropped open.

"It's about respect," I said.

He reached out and put a hand on my shoulder. "You got mine, little brother. You're point guard, you call the play."

I slapped the ball. "Five!" I yelled.

"Five?" Kia questioned.

"You heard me."

Five was an isolation play we ran with our team. It meant that Kia had to break through screens to get open for a quick shot. It was meant as a last-second shot—quick inbounds pass for a quick shot.

JYD, of course, had no idea what the play was, but

knew it was something meant for Kia. As she broke around him, JYD lay down a pick that separated her from Ethan. Ben switched off, racing to keep up to Kia. As she reached her spot, I threw in the pass.

Ben was on top of her instantly, making the shot impossible. She dribbled away and I ran, trying to get open. She threw out a pass and I managed to grab the ball. Instantly I fired it out—high and hard—to JYD. He snared the pass and started to dribble.

I knew how easily he could beat his man. We only needed three points. We could just give him the ball and he could drive a couple of times and win the game for us. That would have been so easy...but easy wasn't necessarily right.

I faded off to the side, trying to slip away as everybody watched JYD handle the ball.

"I'm open!" I screamed at the top of my lungs.

JYD fired the ball to me and everybody became unfrozen at once. Devon and Ethan rushed toward me to block the shot. I bounced a pass underneath their outstretched arms, the ball hitting Kia in the hands. She was standing at the three-point line. She turned, aimed and the ball went up—a perfect shot for the winner!

19

I rushed over to Kia, but JYD got there first. He picked her up and tossed her high into the air—so high that she could have slammed...on the way down! The crowd surged forward from all sides and swept me up in a wave of backslaps, handshakes, laughter and cheers. JYD and I exchanged a high five, and then Kia rushed over and threw her arms around me in a big bear hug!

"We did it!" I screamed as she released me.

"Did you have any doubts?"

"Lots and lots," I admitted.

"Congratulations, Kia. Congratulations, Nick," JYD said. "You did it."

"We did it. We wouldn't have had a chance without you."

"And I wouldn't have had a chance without you two. We did it as a team. Besides, it wasn't just the score that made you two winners. It was the way you played."

"I think we earned their respect," I said.

"You earned the respect of everybody, both on and off the court. You showed how to be real winners."

"They don't look too happy," I said, gesturing to where Ben, Devon and Ethan were standing, off by the fence, gathering up their things.

"Would you be happy?" Kia asked.

"Probably not."

"No shame in losing," JYD said. "You can win with honor and you can lose with honor. Come on, let's go over and tell them 'Good game'."

"Good game and goodbye," Kia said.

"Why goodbye?" JYD asked.

"They have to leave. We won, so they have to go. Whoever won became the kings—and queen—of the court," Kia said. "When they kicked us off, they said that we could come back when we could beat them and then they'd leave...so they're gone...and I can't say that I'm not happy about it."

Judging from the expression on JYD's face, he *was* unhappy.

"Isn't that what a bunch of bullies deserve?" Kia asked, reading his expression. "Doesn't it serve them right to get back what they were giving out?"

JYD didn't answer.

"If they had won, they would have been kicking us off," Kia said.

"Maybe," JYD said. "Nick, are you feeling good about making them leave?"

"I feel good about winning and the way we won," I said.

"That wasn't what I was asking."

"Making them leave is giving them what they gave us, but ... but, I don't know."

"Let's see if I understand. They chase you away because they're bigger and better, and it was wrong. Now, today, we're bigger and better and we're chasing them away, and somehow that's now right?" JYD asked.

"Well ... yeah ... sort of," Kia said.

"Now it just seems like we're being the bullies," JYD said. "How does that feel?"

"Better than being bullied," Kia said.

"But not much better," I added.

"Kia?" JYD asked.

"Okay, not much better ... but I'm not leaving."

"Maybe nobody has to leave," JYD said.

"What do you have in mind?" I asked.

"To get respect you have to give respect. Let's go and talk to them, offer our congratulations to them."

We walked over. The crowd was thinning out, and a few guys were already tossing up shots at the far end of the court.

"Good game," JYD said. He shook Ben's hand and then did the same with Ethan and Devon. "You boys can play some ball."

"I guess not enough," Ethan said.

"My little brother and sister can play some ball too, don't you think?"

"They can play," Ben said.

"How old are you two?" Devon asked.

"I'm eleven," I said. "And Kia will be eleven in September."

"Unbelievable," Devon said. "There's no way I was near that good at that age."

"Probably means they've had some good coaches and teachers," JYD said. "People who showed them how to play, who helped and supported them. Gave them encouragement."

"We've had great coaches," Kia said.

"That makes all the difference," JYD said. "Older and experienced people to help you to rise up."

"I got something for you," Ben said to me. He bent down, reached into his backpack and pulled out a basketball. "Here," he said.

"A ball ... why?"

"He was feeling bad about your ball," Ethan said.

"I meant to kick it over the fence," Ben said. "I didn't mean to have it go under the bus. I'm sorry about that. Here, take this ball to make up for the one I destroyed."

"I can't take your ball," I said. I couldn't believe he was even offering it to me—that wasn't what a bully was supposed to do ... especially after we'd shown them up.

"Sure you can take it. Fair is fair."

Reluctantly I took the ball from him. It was a good ball—leather, regulation size, almost new and just signed by JYD. This was the ball I'd fantasized about kicking over the fence!

"Thanks."

"It's the least I could do. You two are all right," Ben said.

"Thanks." Those words meant more to me than the ball did.

"I hear that because you lost you have to leave," JYD said.

Ben nodded.

"I respect that," JYD said. "You made a deal and you're sticking by it. A man..." he turned to Kia, "a person has to keep their word, even if it's hard."

"Yeah," Devon said. "I'm gonna miss this court."

"But a deal is a deal," JYD said. "Right, Kia?"

"Yeah, right. Unless we make another deal."

"Another deal?" JYD asked. "You boys interested in making another deal?"

"It depends," Ethan said. "Do we have to leave the entire town if we lose a second game?"

"Maybe nobody has to leave anywhere," JYD said. "You interested in hearing this new deal?"

"I am," Ben said.

"We're listening," Devon agreed.

"Nick, why don't you tell them," JYD said.

"Me?"

"You're the man. Go ahead."

"Well... I was thinking... how about if you hang on to your ball, and we could all use it together sometimes when we all play on this court."

"You don't want us to leave?" Ben asked.

I shook my head. "I don't want anybody to leave. I just want to be able to play some ball here some times, that's all. If that would be okay."

"That would be really good," Ethan said.

"Yeah, I could go for that too," Devon agreed.

"Sorry," Ben said. "I don't agree."

"You don't?" I questioned.

"Nope. Not all of it. We can play together, but that ball ... it's still yours. I owe you and I need to pay off that debt. If that's okay with you."

"Yeah, of course it is," I agreed.

"Kia?" JYD asked. "Is this all okay with you too?"

"Sure, fine," she muttered, shaking her head. "We'll be good winners, show them respect, treat them like we want to be treated and all that stuff," she mumbled. I knew she wasn't happy, but she knew this was the right thing to do.

"That's what I was hoping to hear. And I'd like to add something else to the deal," JYD said. "I'd like the three of you," he pointed at Ben, Ethan and Devon, "to make sure that this court is open for everybody. I'd like you to be there for the younger kids to make sure they can play ... maybe share your skills, be good leaders and role models, somebody for them to look up to. Do you think you'd be willing to do that?"

"I think we can handle that," Ben said.

"It might even be fun," Devon added.

"Good. I want you all to know that I'm gonna be coming back to check how things are working."

"You are?"

"Sure. My team opens its season right here in your city. I'm thinking that maybe I could come back out here and play a little ball with you again."

"That would be incredible!" I said.

"And then, after our game, the five of you could be my guests at my game ... I was thinking courtside tickets."

"Courtside ... to an NBA game ... that would be amazing!" I exclaimed along with everybody else.

"So do we have ourselves a deal?" JYD asked.

Everyone yelled out in agreement. Who could complain about a deal like that?

"Here come our parents!" Kia said.

I turned around. My father was driving them all in our van.

"I was wondering where they were," JYD said. "I was also wondering one other thing. How much of what happened do they know?"

I looked at Kia. I was hoping she'd come up with a fancy answer. She didn't say anything. She just looked down at her feet.

"Umm… not a lot."

"You didn't tell them about being bullied, did you?" he asked.

I shook my head.

"I remember being your age when some kids at school were giving me a hard time—picking on me. All I had to do was tell my teacher, or my brother Johnnie, and that would have stopped it. I didn't tell anybody. I felt embarrassed… like it was my fault. You have to promise me two things."

"What things?" Kia asked.

"First, that if this ever happens again—somebody bullying you—that you'll tell your parents or your teachers or somebody who can help."

"That's easy," Kia said. "And if you think about it, we did that this time. We told you."

"What's the second thing?" I asked.

"That you tell your parents what happened. No secrets."

"We'll tell them," I said. "Would it be okay if we talked with them later on tonight."

"Tonight would be good," JYD said. "Oh, and

there's still one more condition. Nothing that difficult." He turned to me. "Nick, every day for the rest of the summer, for twenty minutes, you have to promise me you'll read."

"I can do that too," I agreed, happy that it wasn't something more difficult.

"I'll make sure he does it ... every day!" Kia said. "We'll read together."

"Good, because you know no matter how good you are at playing ball, you still have to read to achieve."

ERIC WALTERS is the author of over thirty-five books for children and Young adults, including the eight books in the best-selling basketball series featuring Nick and Kia.

When not writing and visiting schools, Eric enjoys spending time with his family and playing and coaching basketball. He has such a fertile imagination that he still thinks he could give JYD a challenge if they played another game of one-on-one. Eric lives in Mississauga, Ontario, Canada, with his wife Anita and three children, Christina, Nick and Julia. The character Nick is based on Eric's son Nick. His team, the Mississauga Monarches, won the Ontario Championship and many of the characters in this series, including Jamie, Mark, Jordan, Paul and Tristan are his real team-mates.

Jerome Williams was born in Washington, DC, and grew up in Maryland. He attended Georgetown University on a basketball scholarship and received his BA (Honors) in sociology and theology.

In 1996, Jerome was drafted by the NBA's Detroit Pistons. While in Detroit, Jerome became a hometown hero, giving motivational speeches to both children and adults around the city. His efforts to improve his new city were recognized by the NBA as well as by numerous media outlets. Often referred to as Junk Yard Dog, Jerome developed his own personal mascot to go into Detroit schools and motivate students to just be themselves, listen to their teachers and do their best.

After five seasons with the Pistons, and arguably one of their most popular players, Jerome was traded to the Toronto Raptors. Faced with the challenges of starting over, making new friends and exploring the needs of his new community, Jerome and brother Johnnie launched the JYD Project, a community service initiative that aimed to reach and motivate over 500,000 youth across the United States and Canada (www.jydproject.org).

After three seasons with the Toronto Raptors, Jerome was once again traded away from a city that embraced him and his efforts to serve its youth. Realizing that the only way to maintain his community efforts was to empower his partners to continue, Jerome insisted that his brother Johnnie and Steve "QTMC" Coleman stay behind to complete the mission.

Jerome currently plays for the New York Knicks and anticipates reaching out to the youth in the city as soon as the opportunity presents itself. He remains encouraged by his supporting cast, comprising his three daughters, his youngest brother Joshua, and his wife Nikkollett.

If you'd like to have Johnnie Williams and Steve "QTMC" Coleman visit your school, have your principal contact them at bookjohnnie@aol. com. You can help make the Mission Possible!

Johnnie Williams is a youth activist, columnist and visionary who speaks to thousands of students about setting goals, embracing education, investing in themselves and reaching their personal best by avoiding negative influences, underage drinking, bullying and more.

Johnnie was a standout basketball player until a dunk gone wrong left his elbow shattered. Two operations later his dream of playing professional basketball was over, but his passion to lead youth through positive influence continued to grow. Johnnie serves as founder and executive director of the JYD Project. Working with his brother, Jerome "The Junk Yard Dog" Williams. The JYD Project will bring an inspirational message to more than 500,000 American and Canadian students over a five-year period.

Johnnie resides in Michigan with his wife, where he remains active within his home community, working with the Troy Community Coalition. He believes "the majority of our society's problems are man-made, leaving the power of solution in our hands."

Steve Coleman, a.k.a. "QTMC" (Quest To Make a Change), is a Dogg Pound recording artist who established his career as a teenager when the song "My Buddy," recorded with a five-member rap group, rose to number 1 on Detroit's most popular radio station.

Steve soon realized that his life's purpose was to deliver a positive message of hope to youth all over the world. His inspirational songs and passion for performing have created a demand that has resulted in over 800 shows over the past seventeen years. More than a million viewers at schools, conferences, churches and stadiums have enjoyed his dynamic performances. Through the JYD Project, QTMC continues to bring the "Mission Possible" concert to young people, encouraging them to better handle peer pressure, avoid drugs, respect themselves, rise through adversity, reach for their dreams and stop the bullying.

Basketball Series by Eric Walters

Three on Three
Full Court Press
Hoop Crazy!
Long Shot
Road Trip
Off Season
Underdog

Fiction by Eric Walters

War of the Eagles
(Ruth Schwartz Award)

Caged Eagles
(UNESCO Honorable Mention)

Orca Soundings by Eric Walters

Grind
Juice
Overdrive